OVE · MARRIAGE · LOSS · JOURNEYS

CHILDHOOD

Also in this series

FIRST LOVE
Edited by Paul Bailey

FRIENDSHIP
Edited by Shena Mackay

JOURNEYS
Edited by Charles Nicholl

LOSS
Edited by Elspeth Barker

MARRIAGE
Edited by Elizabeth Jane Howard

CHILDHOOD

EDITED BY

Kate Figes

J. M. Dent London

First published in Great Britain in 1997
by J. M. Dent

A CIP catalogue record for this book is available
from the British Library.

ISBN 0 460 87927 8

Typeset at The Spartan Press Ltd,
Lymington, Hants
Set in 10/11½ Photina
Printed in Great Britain by
Clays Ltd, St Ives plc

J. M. Dent

Weidenfeld & Nicolson
The Orion Publishing Group Ltd
Orion House
5 Upper Saint Martin's Lane
London, WC2H 9EA

CONTENTS

INTRODUCTION

We have a tendency as adults to forget that we were all once children. Childhood is considered as something other, a separate magical, innocent state which has to be protected from the dangers and the cynicism of the adult world. In childhood, our emotions are extreme, swerving from blissful contentment to heartache in a matter of moments when things go wrong. In childhood we live with deep, intangible fears of something terrible happening to us because we are not yet big enough to defend ourselves. In childhood we are constantly aware of our impotence compared to the omnipotence of adults.

The poems, anecdotes, extracts and short stories in this short book capture some of the essence of childhood, the unhappinesses as well as the blissful moments. The anthology is arranged chronologically, beginning with the miracle of a newborn infant, through early childhood, youth and the awareness of the adult world drawing closer; ending with the child that we revisit when we become parents. I have included extracts from some of the classics such as Charles Dickens's *Oliver Twist*, Thomas Hardy's *Jude the Obscure* and Charlotte Brontë's *Jane Eyre*, poems by Wordsworth, Walter de la Mare and Elizabeth Barrett Browning as well as modern work by Blake Morrison, Fergal Keane, Liz Lochhead and Jamaica Kincaid.

All editors of anthologies lament the texts that they have had to exclude and with a book this small it was particularly difficult to have to discard so much. However, I have tried to create a book which can be dipped into, where old friends nuzzle against the new, entertaining with the very special wit of children and reminding us of some of the delights and tragedies born of their ignorance and innocence.

INFANCY

MAURA DOOLEY

'Freight'

I am the ship in which you sail,
little dancing bones,
your passage between the dream
and the waking dream,
your sieve, your pea-green boat.
I'll pay whatever toll your ferry needs.
And you, whose history's already charted
in a rope of cells, be tender to
those other unnamed vessels
who will surprise you one day,
tug-tugging, irresistible,
and pull you out beyond your depth,
where you'll look down, puzzled, amazed.

WILLIAM BLAKE

'Infant Sorrow'

My mother groan'd, my father wept;
Into the dangerous world I leapt,
Helpless, naked, piping loud,
Like a fiend hid in a cloud.

Struggling in my father's hands,
Striving against my swadling bands,
Bound and weary, I thought best
To sulk upon my mother's breast.

JEROME K. JEROME

from *Idle Thoughts of an Idle Fellow*

The bell is rung, and somebody sent to tell nurse to bring down. This is the signal for all the females present to commence talking 'baby', during which time you are left to your own sad thoughts, and to speculations upon the practicability of suddenly recollecting an important engagement, and the likelihood of your being believed if you do. Just when you have concocted an absurdly implausible tale about a man outside, the door opens, and a tall, severe-looking woman enters, carrying what at first sight appears to be a particularly skinny bolster, with the feathers all at one end. Instinct, however, tells you that this is the baby, and you rise with a miserable attempt at appearing eager. When the first gush of feminine enthusiasm with which the object in question is received has died out, and the number of ladies talking at once has been reduced to the ordinary four or five, the circle of fluttering petticoats divides, and room is made for you to step forward. This you do with much the same air that you would walk into the dock at Bow Street, and then, feeling utterly miserable, you stand solemnly staring at the child. There is dead silence, and you know that every one is waiting for you to speak. You try to think of something to say, but find, to your horror, that your reasoning faculties have left you. It is a moment of despair, and your evil genius, seizing the opportunity, suggests to you some of the most idiotic remarks that it is possible for a human being to perpetrate. Glancing round with an imbecile smile, you sniggeringly observe that 'It hasn't got much hair, has it?' Nobody answers you for a minute, but at last the stately nurse says with much gravity – 'It is not customary for children five weeks old to have long hair.'

QUEEN VICTORIA

Letter to the Princess Royal, 2 May 1859

Abstractedly, I have no tendre for them till they have become a little human; an ugly baby is a very nasty object – and the prettiest is frightful when undressed – till about four months; in short as long as they have their big body and little limbs and that terrible frog-like action.

ENID BAGNOLD

from *The Squire* (1938)

The baby was four days old. Now he would come in in the dawn, regally in the midwife's arms, already expectant. He fed greedily at one breast, and as his mother passed him over her body in the darkness to the other he snuffled in a passion of impatience, learning already that there was a second meal, seizing the nipple, choking and sinking to hard-working silence. Sensory exploration which, in the peril of his first day on earth, had centred only in his lips, now spread to his limbs, and his hand, as he worked, from lying stiff like a star, began to move, travelling over the squire's silk nightdress, scratching the silk with his nail in a flurry of his finger, trying the linen sheet, learning the textures. Flinging his hand with a sudden movement behind his head he hit the silver travelling clock. Instantly in the half-light a look of interest broke into his eyes. Letting go, half-turning his head – 'What, what?' his marmoset eyes demanded. But the moment of concentration over he went back to his life's work. All his power was in his lips. His hands were fronds, convolvulus tendrils, catching at surfaces, but only half-informed.

Watching the squire, piercingly sleepless, he would be asleep in a moment.

SU TUNG-P'O (1036–1101)

'On the Birth of His Son'

Families, when a child is born,
Want it to be intelligent.
I, through intelligence,
Having wrecked my whole life,
Only hope the baby will prove
Ignorant and stupid.
Then he will crown a tranquil life
by becoming a Cabinet Minister.

MRS THRALE

from *Diary*, 1777

Dr Collier used to say speaking of Parental Affection that one loved one's Children in Anticipation, one hopes they will one day become useful, estimable, and amiable Beings – one cannot love lumps of Flesh continued he, and they are nothing better during Infancy.

THOMAS HOOD

'A Parental Ode to My Son, Aged Three Years and Five Months' (1837)

Thou happy, happy elf!
(But stop – first let me kiss away that tear)
Thou tiny image of myself!
(My love, he's poking peas into his ear!)
Thou merry, laughing sprite!
With spirits feather-light,
Untouched by sorrow and unsoiled by sin –
(Good heavens, the child is swallowing a pin!)

Thou tricksy Puck!
With antic toys so funnily bestuck,
Light as the singing bird that wings the air –
(The door! the door! he'll tumble down the stair!)
Thou darling of thy sire!
(Why, Jane, he'll set his pinafore a-fire!)
Thou imp of mirth and joy!
In love's dear chain so strong and bright a link,
Thou idol of thy parents – (Drat the boy!
There goes my ink!)

Thou cherub! – but of earth;
Fit playfellow for Fays, by moonlight pale,
In harmless sport and mirth,
(That dog will bite him if he pulls its tail!)

Thou human humming-bee, extracting honey
From every blossom in the world that blows,
Singing in Youth's Elysium every sunny –
(Another tumble! – that's his precious nose!)

Thy father's pride and hope!
(He'll break the mirror with that skipping-rope!)
With pure heart newly stamped from Nature's mint
(Where *did* he learn that squint?)
Thou young domestic dove!
(He'll have that jug off, with another shove!)
Dear nursling of the hymeneal nest!
(Are those torn clothes his best?)
Little epitome of man!
(He'll climb upon the table, that's his plan!)
Touched with the beauteous tints of dawning life –
(He's got a knife!)

Thou enviable being!
No storms, no clouds, in thy blue sky foreseeing,
Play on, play on,
My elfin John!
Toss the light ball – bestride the stick –
(I knew so many cakes would make him sick!)
With fancies buoyant as the thistledown,
Prompting the face grotesque, and antic brisk,
With many a lamblike frisk –
(He's got the scissors, snipping at your gown!)

Thou pretty opening rose!
(Go to your mother, child, and wipe your nose!)
Balmy, and breathing music like the South,
(He really brings my heart into my mouth!)

Fresh as the morn, and brilliant as its star –
(I wish that window had an iron bar!)

Bold as the hawk, yet gentle as the dove –
    (I tell you what, my love,
I cannot write, unless he's sent above!)

EDNA ST VINCENT MILLAY

'Childhood is the Kingdom Where Nobody Dies'

Childhood is not from birth to a certain age and at a certain
age
The child is grown, and puts away childish things,
Childhood is the Kingdom where nobody dies.
Nobody that matters, that is.

ALICE MILLER

from *The Drama of Being a Child*

I was out for a walk and noticed a young couple a few steps ahead, both tall; they had a little boy with them, about two years old, who was running alongside and whining. (We are accustomed to seeing such situations from the adult point of view, but here I want to describe it as it was experienced by the child.) The two had just bought themselves ice-cream bars on sticks from the kiosk and were licking them with enjoyment. The little boy wanted one, too. His mother said affectionately, 'Look, you can have a bite of mine, a whole one is too cold for you.' The child did not want just one bite but held out his hand for the whole ice, which his mother took out of his reach again. He cried in despair, and soon exactly the same thing was repeated with his father: 'There you are, my pet,' said his father affectionately, 'you can have a bite of mine.' 'No, no,' cried the child and ran ahead again, trying to distract himself. Soon he came back again and gazed enviously and sadly up at the two grown-ups who were enjoying their ice-creams contentedly and at one. Time and again he held out his little hand for the whole ice-cream bar, but the adult hand with its treasure was withdrawn again.

The more the child cried, the more it amused his parents. It made them laugh a lot and they hoped to humour him along with their laughter, too: 'Look, it isn't so important, what a fuss you are making.' Once the child sat down on the ground and began to throw little stones over his shoulder in his mother's direction, but then he suddenly got up again and looked around anxiously, making sure that his parents were still there. When his father had completely finished his ice cream, he gave the stick to the child and walked on. The little boy licked the bit of wood expectantly, looked at it, threw it away, wanted to pick it up again but did not do so, and a deep sob of loneliness and disappointment shook his small body. Then he trotted obediently after his parents.

It seemed clear to me that this little boy was not being frustrated by his 'oral drives', for he was given ample opportunity to take a bite; it was his narcissistic needs that were constantly being wounded and frustrated. His wish to hold the ice-cream stick in his hand like the others was not understood; worse still, it was laughed at – they made fun of his needs. He was faced with two giants who were proud of being consistent and also supported each other – while he, quite alone in his distress, obviously could say nothing beyond no, nor could he make himself clear to his parents with his gestures (which were very expressive). He had no advocate.

Why, indeed, did these parents behave with so little empathy? Why didn't one of them think of eating a little quicker or even of throwing away half his ice-cream and giving the child his stick with a bit of edible substance? Why did they both stand there laughing, eating so slowly and showing so little concern about the child's obvious distress? They were not unkind or cold parents; the father spoke to his child very tenderly. Nevertheless, at least at this moment, they displayed a lack of empathy. We can only solve this riddle if we manage to see the parents, too, as insecure children – children who have at last found a weaker creature, and in comparison with him they now can feel very strong. What child has never been laughed at for his fears and been told, 'You don't need to be afraid of a thing like that'? And what child will then not feel shamed and despised because he could not assess the danger correctly, and will that little person not take the next opportunity to pass on these feelings to a still smaller child? Such experiences come in all shades and varieties. Common to them all is the sense of strength that it gives the adult to face the weak and helpless child's fear and to have the possibility of controlling fear in another person, while he cannot control his own.

No doubt, in twenty years' time, or perhaps earlier, if he has younger siblings, our little boy will replay this scene with the ice-cream, but then *he* will be in possession and the other one will be the helpless, envious, weak little creature, whom he then no longer has to carry within himself, but now can split off and project outside himself.

CHARLIE BAKUS

'My Baby'

I'm the father of an infant,
  Baby mine, baby mine;
He won't let me rest an instant,
  Baby mine, baby mine;
He won't do a thing he's bid,
How I wish that I was rid
Of that awful sassy kid,
  Baby mine, baby mine,
Of that awful sassy kid,
  Baby mine.

At my meals I have to hold him,
  Baby mine, baby mine;
But I never dare to scold him,
  Baby mine, baby mine;
My face he'll surely scratch,
And the tablecloth he'll snatch,
All my crockery goes smash,
  Baby mine, baby mine,
All my crockery goes smash,
  Baby mine.

In my hair he often lingers,
  Baby mine, baby mine;

With molasses on his fingers,
Baby mine, baby mine;
You ought to hear him roar,
While I have to walk the floor,
Oh, I'd like to break his jaw,
Baby mine, baby mine,
Yes, I'd like to break his jaw,
Baby mine.

Sung by Charlie Backus at
the San Francisco Minstrels
opera house, c. 1880.

CHRISTY BROWN

from *My Left Foot*

I was born in the Rotunda Hospital, on 5 June 1932. There were nine children before me and twelve after me, so I myself belong to the middle group. Out of this total of twenty-two, seventeen lived, four died in infancy, leaving thirteen still to hold the family fort.

Mine was a difficult birth, I am told. Both mother and son almost died. A whole army of relations queued up outside the hospital until the small hours of the morning, waiting for news and praying furiously that it would be good.

After my birth mother was sent to recuperate for some weeks and I was kept in the hospital while she was away. I remained there for some time, without name, for I wasn't baptized until my mother was well enough to bring me to church.

It was mother who first saw that there was something wrong with me. I was about four months old at the time. She noticed that my head had a habit of falling backwards whenever she tried to feed me. She attempted to correct this by placing her hand on the back of my neck to keep it steady. But when she took it away back it would drop again. That was the first warning sign. Then she became aware of other defects as I got older. She saw that my hands were clenched nearly all of the time and were inclined to twine behind my back; my mouth couldn't grasp the teat of the bottle because even at that early age my jaws would either lock together tightly, so that it was impossible for her to open them, or they would suddenly become limp and fall loose, dragging my whole mouth to one side. At six months I could not sit up without having a mountain of pillows around me; at twelve months it was the same.

Very worried by this, mother told my father her fears, and they decided to seek medical advice without any further delay. I was little over a year old when they began to take me to hospitals and clinics, convinced that there was something definitely wrong with me, something which they could not understand or name, but which was very real and disturbing.

Almost every doctor who saw and examined me labelled me a very interesting but also a hopeless case. Many told mother very gently that I was mentally defective and would remain so. That was a hard blow to a young mother who had already reared five healthy children. The doctors were so very sure of themselves that mother's faith in me seemed almost an impertinence. They assured her that nothing could be done for me.

She refused to accept this truth, the inevitable truth – as it then seemed – that I was beyond cure, beyond saving, even beyond hope. She could not and would not believe that I was an imbecile, as the doctors told her. She had nothing in the world to go by, not a scrap of evidence to support her conviction that, though my body was crippled, my mind was not. In spite of all the doctors and specialists told her, she would not agree. I don't believe she knew why – she just knew without feeling the smallest shade of doubt.

Finding that the doctors could not help in any way beyond telling her not to place her trust in me, or, in other words, to forget I was a human creature, rather to regard me as just something to be fed and washed and then put away again, mother decided there and then to take matters into her own hands. I was *her* child, and therefore part of the family. No matter how dull and incapable I might grow up to be, she was determined to treat me on the same plane as the others, and not as the 'queer one' in the back room who was never spoken of when there were visitors present.

That was a momentous decision as far as my future life was concerned. It meant that I would always have my mother on my side to help me fight all the battles that were to come, and to inspire me with new strength when I was almost beaten. But it wasn't easy for her because now the relatives and friends had decided otherwise. They contended that I should be taken kindly, sympathetically, but not seriously. That would be a mistake. 'For your own sake,' they told her, 'don't look to this boy as you would to the others; it would only break your heart in the end.' Luckily for me, mother and father held out against the lot of them. But mother wasn't content just to say that I was not an idiot; she set out to prove it, not because of any rigid sense of duty, but out of love. That is why she was so successful.

At this time she had the five other children to look after besides the 'difficult one', though as yet it was not by any means a full house. There were my brothers, Jim, Tony and Paddy, and my two sisters, Lily and Mona, all of them very young, just a year or so between each of them, so that they were almost exactly like steps of stairs.

Four years rolled by and I was now five, and still as helpless as a newly born baby. While my father was out at bricklaying earning our bread and butter for us, mother was slowly, patiently pulling down the wall, brick by brick, that seemed to thrust itself between me and the other children, slowly, patiently penetrating beyond the thick curtain that hung over my mind, separating it from theirs. It was hard, heartbreaking work, for often all she got from me in return was a vague smile and perhaps a faint gurgle. I could not speak or even mumble, nor could I sit up without support on my own, let alone take steps. But I wasn't inert or motionless, I seemed indeed to be convulsed with movement, wild, stiff, snake-like movement that never left me, except in sleep. My fingers twisted and twitched continually, my arms twined backwards and would often shoot out suddenly this way and that, and my head lolled and sagged sideways. I was a queer, crooked little fellow.

Mother tells me how one day she had been sitting with me for hours in an upstairs room, showing me pictures out of a great big storybook that I had got from Santa Claus last Christmas and telling me the names of the different animals and flowers that were in them, trying without success to get me to repeat them. This had gone on for hours while she talked and laughed with me. Then at the end of it she leaned over me and said gently into my ear:

'Did you like it, Chris? Did you like the bears and the monkeys and all the lovely flowers? Nod your head for yes, like a good boy.'

But I could make no sign that I had understood her. Her face was bent over mine, hopefully. Suddenly, involuntarily, my queer hand reached up and grasped one of the dark curls that fell in a thick cluster about her neck. Gently she loosened the clenched fingers, though some dark strands were still clutched between them.

Then she turned away from my curious stare and left the room, crying. The door closed behind her. It all seemed hopeless. It looked as though there was some justification for my relatives' contention that I was an idiot and beyond help.

They now spoke of an institution.

'Never!' said my mother almost fiercely, when this was suggested to her. 'I know my boy is not an idiot. It is his body that is shattered, not his mind. I'm sure of that.'

Sure? Yet inwardly, she prayed God would give her some proof of her faith. She knew it was one thing to believe but quite another thing to prove.

I was now five, and still I showed no real sign of intelligence. I showed no apparent interest in things except with my toes – more especially those of my left foot. Although my natural habits were clean I could not aid myself, but in this respect my father took care of me. I used to lie on my back all the time in the kitchen or, on bright warm days, out in the garden, a little bundle of crooked muscles and twisted nerves, surrounded by a family that loved me and hoped for me and that made me part of their own warmth and humanity. I was lonely, imprisoned in a world of my own, unable to communicate with others, cut off, separated from them as though a glass wall stood between my existence and theirs, thrusting me beyond the sphere of their lives and activities. I longed to run about and play with the rest, but I was unable to break loose from my bondage.

Then, suddenly, it happened! In a moment everything was changed, my future life moulded into a definite shape, my mother's faith in me rewarded and her secret fear changed into open triumph.

It happened so quickly, so simply after all the years of waiting and uncertainty that I can see and feel the whole scene as if it had happened last week. It was the afternoon of a cold, grey December day. The streets outside glistened with snow; the white sparkling flakes stuck and melted on the windowpanes and hung on the boughs of the trees like molten silver. The wind howled dismally, whipping up little whirling columns of snow that rose and fell at every fresh gust. And over all, the dull, murky sky stretched like a dark canopy, a vast infinity of greyness.

Inside, all the family were gathered round the big kitchen fire that lit up the little room with a warm glow and made giant shadows dance on the walls and ceiling.

In a corner Mona and Paddy were sitting huddled together, a few torn school primers before them. They were writing down little sums on to an old chipped slate, using a bright piece of yellow chalk. I was close to them, propped up by a few pillows against the wall, watching.

It was the chalk that attracted me so much. It was a long, slender stick of vivid yellow. I had never seen anything like it before, and it showed up so well against the black surface of the slate that I was fascinated by it as much as if it had been a stick of gold.

Suddenly I wanted desperately to do what my sister was

doing. Then – without thinking or knowing exactly what I was doing, I reached out and took the stick of the chalk out of my sister's hand – *with my left foot.*

I do not know why I used my left foot to do this. It is a puzzle to many people as well as to myself, for, although I had displayed a curious interest in my toes at an early age, I had never attempted before this to use either of my feet in any way. They could have been as useless to me as were my hands. That day, however, my left foot, apparently on its own volition, reached out and very impolitely took the chalk out of my sister's hand.

I held it tightly between my toes, and, acting on an impulse, made a wild sort of scribble with it on the slate. Next moment I stopped, a bit dazed, surprised, looking down at the stick of yellow chalk stuck between my toes, not knowing what to do with it next, hardly knowing how it got there. Then I looked up and became aware that everyone had stopped talking and was staring at me silently. Nobody stirred. Mona, her black curls framing her chubby little face, stared at me with great big eyes and open mouth. Across the open hearth, his face lit by flames, sat my father, leaning forward, hands outspread on his knees, his shoulders tense. I felt the sweat break out on my forehead.

My mother came in from the pantry with a steaming pot in her hand. She stopped midway between the table and the fire, feeling the tension flowing through the room. She followed their stare and saw me, in the corner. Her eyes looked from my face down to my foot, with the chalk gripped between my toes. She put down the pot.

Then she crossed over to me and knelt down beside me, as she had done so many times before.

'I'll show you what to do with it, Chris,' she said, very slowly and in a queer, jerky way, her face flushed as if with some inner excitement.

Taking another piece of chalk from Mona, she hesitated, then very deliberately drew, on the floor in front of me, *the single letter 'A'.*

'Copy that,' she said, looking steadily at me. 'Copy it, Christy.'

I couldn't.

I looked about me, looked around at the faces that were turned towards me, tense, excited faces that were at that moment frozen, immobile, eager, waiting for a miracle in their midst.

The stillness was profound. The room was full of flame and shadow that danced before my eyes and lulled my taut nerves into a sort of waking sleep. I could hear the sound of the water-tap dripping in the pantry, the loud ticking of the clock on the mantelshelf, and the soft hiss and crackle of the logs on the open hearth.

I tried again. I put out my foot and made a wild jerking stab with the chalk which produced a very crooked line and nothing more. Mother held the slate steady for me.

'Try again, Chris,' she whispered in my ear. 'Again.'

I did. I stiffened my body and put my left foot out again, for the third time. I drew one side of the letter. I drew half the other side. Then the stick of chalk broke and I was left with a stump. I wanted to fling it away and give up. Then I felt my mother's hand on my shoulder. I tried once more. Out went my foot. I shook, I sweated and strained every muscle. My hands were so tightly clenched that my fingernails bit into the flesh. I set my teeth so hard that I nearly pierced my lower lip. Everything in the room swam till the faces around me were mere patches of white. But – I drew it – *the letter 'A'*. There it was on the floor before me. Shaky, with awkward, wobbly sides and a very uneven centre line. But it *was* the letter 'A'. I looked up. I saw my mother's face for a moment, tears on her cheeks. Then my father stooped down and hoisted me on to his shoulder.

I had done it! It had started – the thing that was to give my mind its chance of expressing itself. True, I couldn't speak with my lips, but now I would speak through something more lasting than spoken words – written words.

That one letter, scrawled on the floor with a broken bit of yellow chalk gripped between my toes, was my road to a new world, my key to mental freedom. It was to provide a source of relaxation to the tense, taut thing that was me which panted for expression behind a twisted mouth.

A. E. HOUSMAN

'The Grizzly Bear is huge and wild'

The Grizzly Bear is huge and wild;
He has devoured the infant child.
The infant child is not aware
It has been eaten by the bear.

CHILDHOOD

OGDEN NASH

'Baby, What Makes the Sky Blue?'

Sophisticated parents live agog in a world that to them is
enchanted;
Ingenious children just naively take it for granted.

JOHN BETJEMAN

from *Summoned by Bells*

Childhood is measured out by sounds and smells
And sights before the dark of reason grows.

ALAN BENNETT

from *Forty Years On*

(Nanny Gibbons is played by Matron, and is a much more intimidating presence than Nursie. At first only a voice behind the screen, she casts a monstrous shadow on the wall as she unbuckles her black bombazine armour and talks to the little boy in the bed.)

BOY What time is it, Nanny?
NANNY Time you were asleep, young man.
BOY What time is it?
NANNY Time you had a watch. Time you learned to say please. Time you knew better. Go to sleep.
BOY What you are doing, Nanny?
NANNY I'm doing what I'm doing. Go to sleep.
BOY Nanny!
NANNY What?
BOY I've got a pain in my leg.
NANNY Do you wonder you've got pains in your legs when you don't do your business. Well next time you'll sit there till you do. Forgotten to fold your vest, young man. I can't turn my back for two minutes. And clean on this afternoon.
BOY I feel sick.
NANNY Do you wonder you feel sick sitting on them hot pipes. How many more times must I tell you, you sit on them pipes you'll catch piles.

BOY What are piles?

NANNY You mind your own business. Piles is piles, and you'll know soon enough when you catch them because your insides'll drop out and you'll die and then where will you be? Lie down, sitting up at this time of night.

BOY What time is it?

NANNY Time for Bedfordshire. Time you had your bottom smacked.

BOY Can I have an apple?

NANNY No you can't. Apples at this time of night. Apples don't grow on trees you know. (*She has a drink from a bottle.*)

BOY What's that?

NANNY That's Nanny's medicine.

BOY What for?

NANNY It's for Nanny's leg. Nanny's got a bone in her leg.

BOY Can I have some for my leg?

NANNY No, you can't. Going out without your wellies on, do you wonder you get pains in your legs. You go out without your wellies on, you'll go blind. That's why St Paul went blind. Went out on the Damascus Road without his wellies on. See, did I say no? Lie down this minute. If I have another snuff out of you there'll be ructions. Give me a kiss. Kisses make babies grow. Night, night, sleep tight. God bless and go to sleep or the policeman'll come and cut your little tail off.

ANITA DESAI

'Games at Twilight'

It was still too hot to play outdoors. They had had their tea, they had been washed and had their hair brushed, and after the long day of confinement in the house that was not cool but at least a protection from the sun, the children strained to get out. Their faces were red and bloated with the effort, but their mother would not open the door, everything was still curtained and shuttered in a way that stifled the children, made them feel that their lungs were stuffed with cotton wool and their noses with dust and if they didn't burst out into the light and see the sun and feel the air, they would choke.

'Please, ma, please,' they begged. 'We'll play in the veranda and porch – we won't go a step out of the porch.'

'You will, I know you will, and then—'

'No – we won't, we won't,' they wailed so horrendously that she actually let down the bolt of the front door so that they burst out like seeds from a crackling, over-ripe pod into the veranda, with such wild, maniacal yells that she retreated to her bath and the shower of talcum powder and the fresh sari that were to help her face the summer evening.

They faced the afternoon. It was too hot. Too bright. The white walls of the veranda glared stridently in the sun. The bougainvillea hung about it, purple and magenta, in livid balloons. The garden outside was like a tray made of beaten brass, flattened out on the red gravel and the stony soil in all shades of metal – aluminium, tin, copper and brass. No life stirred at this arid time of day – the birds still drooped, like dead fruit, in the papery tents of the trees; some squirrels lay limp on the wet earth under the garden tap. The outdoor dog lay stretched as if dead on the veranda mat, his paws and ears and tail all reaching out like dying travellers in search of water. He rolled his eyes at the children – two white marbles rolling in the purple sockets, begging for sympathy – and attempted to lift his tail in a wag but could not. It only twitched and lay still.

Then, perhaps roused by the shrieks of the children, a band of parrots suddenly fell out of the eucalyptus tree, tumbled frantically in the still, sizzling air, then sorted themselves out into battle formation and streaked away across the white sky.

The children, too, felt released. They too began tumbling, shoving, pushing against each other, frantic to start. Start what? Start their business. The business of the children's day which is – play.

'Let's play hide-and-seek.'

'Who'll be It?'

'You be It.'

'Why should I? You be—'

'You're the eldest—'

'That doesn't mean—'

The shoves became harder. Some kicked out. The motherly Mira intervened. She pulled the boys roughly apart. There was a tearing sound of cloth but it was lost in the heavy panting and angry grumbling and no one paid attention to the small sleeve hanging loosely off a shoulder.

'Make a circle, make a circle!' she shouted, firmly pulling and pushing till a kind of vague circle was formed. 'Now clap!' she roared and, clapping, they all chanted in melancholy unison: 'Dip, dip, dip – my blue ship—' and every now and then one or the other saw he was safe by the way his hands fell at the crucial moment – palm on palm, or back of hand on palm – and dropped out of the circle with a yell and a jump of relief and jubilation.

Raghu was It. He started to protest, to cry 'You cheated – Mira cheated – Anu cheated—' but it was too late, the others had all already streaked away. There was no one to hear when he called out, 'Only in the veranda – the porch – Ma said – Ma *said* to stay in the porch!' No one had stopped to listen, all he saw were their brown legs flashing through the dusty shrubs, scrambling up brick walls, leaping over compost heaps and hedges, and then the porch stood empty in the purple shade of the bougainvillea and the garden was as empty as before; even the limp squirrels had whisked away, leaving everything gleaming, brassy and bare.

Only small Manu suddenly reappeared, as if he had dropped out of an invisible cloud or from a bird's claws, and stood for a moment in the centre of the yellow lawn, chewing his finger and near to tears as he heard Raghu shouting, with his head pressed against the veranda wall, 'Eighty-three, eighty-five, eighty-nine, ninety . . .' and then made off in a panic, half of him wanting to fly north, the other half counselling south. Raghu turned just in time to see the flash of his white shorts and the uncertain skittering of his red sandals, and charged after him with such a blood-curdling yell that Manu stumbled over the hosepipe, fell into its rubber coils and lay there weeping, 'I won't be It – you have to find them all – all – All!'

'I know I have to, idiot,' Raghu said, superciliously kicking him with his toe. 'You're dead,' he said with satisfaction, licking the beads of perspiration off his upper lip, and then stalked off in search of worthier prey, whistling spiritedly so that the hiders should hear and tremble.

Ravi heard the whistling and picked his nose in a panic, trying to find comfort by burrowing the finger deep – deep into that soft tunnel. He felt himself too exposed, sitting on an upturned flower pot behind the garage. Where could he burrow? He could run around the garage if he heard Raghu come – around and around and around – but he hadn't much faith in his short legs when matched against Raghu's long, hefty, hairy footballer legs. Ravi had a frightening glimpse of them as Raghu combed the hedge of crotons and hibiscus, trampling delicate ferns underfoot as he did so. Ravi looked about him desperately, swallowing a small ball of snot in his fear.

The garage was locked with a great heavy lock to which the driver had the key in the room, hanging from a nail on the wall under his workshirt. Ravi had peeped in and seen him still sprawling on his string-cot in his vest and striped underpants, the hair on his chest and the hair in his nose shaking with the vibrations of his phlegm-obstructed snores. Ravi had wished he were tall enough, big enough to reach the key on the nail, but it was impossible, beyond his reach for years to come. He had sidled away and sat dejectedly on the flower pot. That at least was cut to his own size.

But next to the garage was another shed with a big green door. Also locked. No one even knew who had the key to the lock. That shed wasn't opened more than once a year when Ma turned out all the old broken bits of furniture and rolls of matting and leaking buckets, and the white ant hills were broken and swept away and Flit sprayed into the spider webs and rat holes so that the whole operation was like the looting of a poor, ruined and conquered city. The green leaves of the door sagged. They were nearly off their rusty hinges. The hinges were large and made a small gap between the door and the walls – only just large enough for rats, dogs and, possibly, Ravi to slip through.

Ravi had never cared to enter such a dark and depressing mortuary of defunct household goods seething with such unspeakable and alarming animal life but, as Raghu's whistling grew angrier and sharper and his crashing and storming in the hedge wilder, Ravi suddenly slipped off the flower pot and through the crack and was gone. He chuckled aloud with astonishment at his own temerity so that Raghu came out of the hedge, stood silent with his hands on his hips, listening, and finally shouted, 'I heard you! I'm coming! *Got* you—' and came charging round the garage only to find the upturned flower pot, the yellow dust, the crawling of white ants in a mud-hill against the closed shed door – nothing. Snarling, he bent to pick up a stick and went off, whacking it against the garage and shed walls as if to beat out his prey.

Ravi shook, then shivered with delight, with self-congratulation. Also with fear. It was dark, spooky in the shed. It had a muffled smell, as of graves. Ravi had once got locked into the linen cupboard and sat there weeping for half an hour before he was rescued. But at least that had been a familiar place, and even smelt pleasantly of starch, laundry and, reassuringly, of his mother. But the shed smelt of rats, ant hills, dust and spider webs. Also of less definable, less recognizable horrors. And it was dark. Except for the white-hot cracks along the door, there was no light. The roof was very low. Although Ravi was small, he felt as if he could reach up and touch it with his finger tips. But he didn't stretch. He hunched himself into a ball so as not to bump into anything. What might there not be to touch him and feel him as he stood there, trying to see in the dark? Something cold, or slimy – like a snake. Snakes! He leapt up as Raghu whacked the wall with his stick – then, quickly realizing what it was, felt almost relieved to hear Raghu, hear his stick. It made him feel protected.

But Raghu soon moved away. There wasn't a sound once his footsteps had gone around the garage and disappeared. Ravi stood frozen inside the shed. Then he shivered all over. Something had tickled the back of his neck. It took him a while to pick up the courage to lift his hand and explore. It was an insect – perhaps a spider – exploring *him*. He squashed it and wondered how many more creatures were watching him, waiting to reach out and touch him, the stranger.

There was nothing now. After standing in that position – his hand still on his neck, feeling the wet splodge of the squashed spider gradually dry – for minutes, hours, his legs began to tremble with the effort, the inaction. By now he could see enough in the dark to make out the large solid shapes of old wardrobes, broken buckets and bedsteads piled on top of each other around him. He recognized an old bathtub – patches of enamel glimmered at him and at last he lowered himself on to its edge.

He contemplated slipping out of the shed and into the fray. He wondered if it would not be better to be captured by Raghu and be returned to the milling crowd as long as he could be in the sun, the light, the free spaces of the garden and the familiarity of his brothers, sisters and cousins. It would be evening soon. Their games would become legitimate. The parents would sit out on the lawn on cane basket chairs and watch them as they tore around the garden or gathered in knots to share a loot of mulberries or black, teeth-splitting *jamun* from the garden trees. The gardener would fix the hosepipe to the water tap and water would fall lavishly through the air to the ground, soaking the dry yellow grass and the red gravel and arousing the sweet, the intoxicating scent of water on dry earth – that loveliest scent in the world. Ravi sniffed for a whiff of it. He half-rose from the bathtub, then heard the despairing scream of one of the girls as Raghu bore down upon her. There was the sound of a crash, and of rolling about in the bushes, the shrubs, then screams and accusing sobs of, 'I touched the den—' 'You did not—' 'I did—' 'You liar, you did *not*' and then a fading away and silence again.

Ravi sat back on the harsh edge of the tub, deciding to hold out a bit longer. What fun if they were all found and caught – he alone left unconquered! He had never known that sensation. Nothing more wonderful had ever happened to him than being taken out by an uncle and bought a whole slab of chocolate all to himself, or being flung into the soda-man's pony cart and driven up to the gate by the friendly driver with the red beard and pointed ears. To defeat Raghu – that hirsute, hoarse-voiced football champion – and to be the winner in a circle of older, bigger, luckier children – that would be thrilling beyond imagination. He hugged his knees together and smiled to himself almost shyly at the thought of so much victory, such laurels.

There he sat smiling, knocking his heels against the bath-tub, now and then getting up and going to the door to put his ear to the broad crack and listening for sounds of the game, the pursuer and the pursued, and then returning to his seat with the dogged determination of the true winner, a breaker of records, a champion.

It grew darker in the shed as the light at the door grew softer, fuzzier, turned to a kind of crumbling yellow pollen that turned to yellow fur, blue fur, grey fur. Evening. Twilight. The sound of water gushing, falling. The scent of earth receiving water, slaking its thirst in great gulps and releasing that green scent of freshness, coolness. Through the crack Ravi saw the long purple shadows of the shed and the garage lying still across the yard. Beyond that, the white walls of the house. The bougainvillea had lost its lividity, hung in dark bundles that quaked and twittered and seethed with masses of homing sparrows. The lawn was shut off from his view. Could he hear the children's voices? It seemed to him that he could. It seemed to him that he could hear them chanting, singing, laughing. But what about the game? What had happened? Could it be over? How could it when he was still not found?

It then occurred to him that he could have slipped out long ago, dashed across the yard to the veranda and touched the 'den'. It was necessary to do that to win. He had forgotten. He had only remembered the part of hiding and trying to elude the seeker. He had done that so successfully, his success had occupied him so wholly that he had quite forgotten that success had to be clinched by that final dash to victory and the ringing cry of 'Den!'

With a whimper he burst through the crack, fell on his knees, got up and stumbled on stiff, benumbed legs across the shadowy yard, crying heartily by the time he reached the veranda so that when he flung himself at the white pillar and bawled, 'Den! Den! Den!' his voice broke with rage and pity at the disgrace of it all and he felt himself flooded with tears and misery.

Out on the lawn, the children stopped chanting. They all turned to stare at him in amazement. Their faces were pale and triangular in the dusk. The trees and bushes around them stood inky and sepulchral, spilling long shadows across them. They stared, wondering at his reappearance, his passion, his wild animal howling. Their mother rose from her basket chair and came towards him, worried, annoyed, saying, 'Stop it, stop it, Ravi. Don't be a baby. Have you hurt yourself?' Seeing him attended to, the children went back to clasping their hands and chanting 'The grass is green, the rose is red . . .'

But Ravi would not let them. He tore himself out of his mother's grasp and pounded across the lawn into their midst, charging at them with his head lowered so that they scattered in surprise. 'I won, I won, I won,' he bawled, shaking his head so that the big tears flew. 'Raghu didn't find me. I won, I won—'

It took them a minute to grasp what he was saying, even who he was. They had quite forgotten about him. Raghu had found all the others long ago. There had been a fight about who was to be It next. It had been so fierce that their mother had emerged from her bath and made them change to another game. Then they had played another and another. Broken mulberries from the tree and eaten them. Helped the driver wash the car when their father returned from work. Helped the gardener water the beds till he roared at them and swore he would complain to their parents. The parents had come out, taken up their positions on the cane chairs. They had begun to play again, sing and chant. All this time no one had remembered Ravi. Having disappeared from the scene, he had disappeared from their minds. Clean.

'Don't be a fool,' Raghu said roughly, pushing him aside, and even Mira said, 'Stop howling, Ravi. If you want to play, you can stand at the end of the line,' and she put him there very firmly.

The game proceeded. Two pairs of arms reached up and met in an arc. The children trooped under it again and again in a lugubrious circle, ducking their heads and intoning

'The grass is green,
The rose is red;
Remember me
When I am dead, dead, dead, dead . . .'

And the arc of thin arms trembled in the twilight, and the heads were bowed so sadly, and their feet tramped to that melancholy refrain so mournfully, so helplessly, that Ravi could not bear it. He would not follow them, he would not be included in this funereal game. He had wanted victory and triumph – not a funeral. But he had been forgotten, left out and he would not join them now. The ignominy of being forgotten – how could he face it? He felt his heart go heavy and ache inside him unbearably. He lay down full length on the damp grass, crushing his face into it, no longer crying, silenced by the terrible sense of his insignificance.

ANONYMOUS

from *A Young Girl's Diary*, 1921

24 July. Today is Sunday. I do love Sundays. Father says: You children have Sundays every day. That's quite true in the holidays, but not at other times. The peasants and their wives and children are all very gay, wearing Tyrolese dresses, just like those I have seen in the theatre. We are wearing our white dresses today, and I have made a great cherry stain upon mine, not on purpose, but because I sat down upon some fallen cherries. So this afternoon when we go out walking I must wear my pink dress. All the better, for I don't care to be dressed exactly the same as Dora. I don't see why everyone should know that we are sisters. Let people think we are cousins. She does not like it either; I wish I knew why. Oswald is coming in a week, and I am awfully pleased. He is older than Dora, but I can always get on with him. Hella writes that she finds it dull without me; so do I.

25 July. I wrote to Fraülein Prückl today. She is staying at Achensee. I should like to see her. Every afternoon we bathe and then go for a walk. But today it has been raining all day. Such a bore. I forgot to bring my paint-box and I'm not allowed to read all day. Mother says, If you gobble all your books up now you'll have nothing left to read. That's quite true, but I can't even go and swing.

Afternoon. I must write some more. I've had a frightful row with Dora. She says I've been fiddling with her things.

It's all because she's so untidy. As if *her* things could interest me. Yesterday she left her letter to Erika lying about on the table, and all I read was: 'He's as handsome as a Greek god.' I don't know who 'he' was for she came in at that moment. It's probably Krail Rudi, with whom she is everlastingly playing tennis and carries on like anything. As for handsome – well, there's no accounting for tastes.

26 July. It's a good thing I brought my dolls' portmanteau. Mother said: You'll be glad to have it on rainy days. Of course I'm much too old to play with dolls, but even though I'm eleven I can make dolls' clothes still. One learns something while one is doing it and when I've finished something I do enjoy it so. Mother cut me out some things, and I was tacking them together. Then Dora came into the room and said: 'Hullo, the child is sewing things for her dolls.' Besides, I don't really play with dolls any longer. When she sat down beside me I sewed so vigorously that I made a great scratch on her hand, and said: 'Oh, I'm so sorry, but you came too close.' I hope she'll know why I really did it. Of course she'll go and sneak to Mother. Let her. What right has she to call me child? She's got a fine red scratch anyhow, and on her right hand where everyone can see.

27 July. There's such a lot of fruit here. I eat raspberries and gooseberries all day and Mother says that is why I have no appetite for dinner. But Dr Klein always says fruit is so wholesome; so why should it be unwholesome all at once? Hella always says that when one likes anything awfully much one is always scolded about it until one gets perfectly sick of it. Hella often gets in such a temper with her mother, and then her mother says: We make such sacrifices for our children and they reward us with ingratitude. I should like to know what sacrifices they make. I think it's the children who make the sacrifices. When I want to eat gooseberries and am not allowed to, the sacrifice is *mine* not *Mother's*.

DYLAN THOMAS

from *Portrait of the Artist as a Young Dog*

On my haunches, eager and alone, casting an ebony shadow, with the Gorsehill jungle swarming, the violent, impossible birds and fishes leaping, hidden under four-stemmed flowers the height of horses, in the early evening in a dingle near Carmarthen, my friend Jack Williams invisibly near me, I felt all my young body like an excited animal surrounding me, the torn knees bent, the bumping heart, the long heat and depth between the legs, the sweat prickling the hands, the tunnels down to the eardrums, the little balls of dirt between the toes, the eyes in the sockets, the tucked up voice, the blood racing, the memory around and within flying, jumping, swimming, and waiting to pounce. There, playing Indians in the evening, I was aware of me myself in the exact middle of a living story, and my body was my adventure and my name. I sprang with excitement and scrambled up through the scratching brambles again.

Jack cried: 'I see you! I see you!' He scampered after me. 'Bang! bang! you're dead!' But I was young and loud and alive, though I lay down obediently.

BLAKE MORRISON

From *And When Did You Last See Your Father?*

The Thursday of Whit week, my parents' afternoon off. On days like this, school holidays or bank holidays, we often drive up the Dales: drystone walls, no trees, and a wind whistling like winter in the telegraph wires. But today it's sunny and we've stayed in the valley, and now we're pulling into the car park, very crowded, at Bolton Abbey. A brown river churfles past the ruin. A line of stones picks its way across – silver buttons on a dead man's chest. Trout leap out of their bull's-eyes to snatch up flies. I ask if we can get out and play here, but my father says, 'No, let's find somewhere quieter,' and off we go, past the Strid (just a step across the churning water, but if you slip you never come up again) and on towards Burnsall. My mother has gone shopping in Harrogate. Auntie Beaty is with us instead.

She's not my real Auntie, but my father calls her that because he says she is almost family. He met her three or four years ago, when she and her husband Sam became managers of the golf club. When my parents go to pubs, my sister and I have to stay in the car, with lemonade and crisps. But at the golf club we can wander off down the fairways looking for lost balls, or play in the yard at the back. I like the yard, the crates of empties stacked under the steamy kitchen window, the wasps you have to mind out for in the orangeades and Britvics. My parents stay a very long time inside, at the bar, where Auntie Beaty or Uncle

Sam serves them. Once everyone was very merry and invited us in and we had shandy, and also onion and sugar sandwiches, which are much nicer than you think they're going to be.

When he has time for a round of golf as well as the bar, my father lets me caddy for him. I wheel his trolley over the frizzed grass, past larks' nests, the ball like a tiny white ulcer in the mouth of a bunker or green. There is one hole, the sixth, where we always see a lapwing, also known as a peewit or plover says the *Observer Book of Birds*. It's a lovely black and white colour, with a crest like one of Auntie Beaty's black curls. When we trundle the clubs past, it flies up, making terrible cries, as if it had been hurt or had lost something, and then suddenly it crashes to the ground and rolls and flops about with a broken wing. My father says not to be fooled, that it's perfect healthy and knows what it's doing, and all its playacting is for just one thing – to lead us away from the nest. Once it flew straight at Uncle Gordon's head when he hit his second shot into the rough – he had got too close to the nest and it was desperate to scare him off.

'Why do we spend so much time with Auntie Beaty?' I asked once when we were driving back over the moors.

'Because she's a bit sad, and needs help,' he said.

'Why?'

'For one thing, she and Uncle Sam can't have children. And they also have money troubles.'

'Do you give them money?'

'I help with their accounts, so they'll learn to understand money and look after it themselves.'

But they can't have learnt to look after money yet, because he is still there most nights till very late, and today Auntie Beaty has come out driving with us, and is sitting in the front of the car holding Josephine while my sister Gill and I sit in the back. Josephine – Josie – is nearly two now, and noisy, and has red cheeks and curly black hair. I can remember the day she was born. My father took my sister and me along to the maternity hospital, Cawder Ghyll: we couldn't go in, so he held us high at the window nearest Auntie Beaty's bed on the ground floor, and we saw the cot with the black head in it. Josie had been a surprise, and my father said we didn't have to feel sorry for Auntie Beaty and Uncle Sam any more: their troubles might not be over, but they had children now, which was a blessing. My mother wasn't there that day, though Cawder Ghull was the hospital she delivered babies at, and she had delivered Josie too.

Auntie Beaty comes to our house a lot. Once I walked into the bathroom when she was feeding Josie: it felt funny, as if I shouldn't be there, but she didn't mind, and I saw her big white breast and the brown nipple when Josie took her mouth away. Another day she brought her Dad with her, Josie's grandpa: he stood at the edge of the raised bottom lawn, where the aubrietia climbs up the wall on to the paved edgings, and suddenly he tipped backwards and fell on his back on the gravel three feet below. He lay there, flat and white and gasping like a fish, and Auntie Beaty screamed, but my father came running with his little bag and helped him up and said it was all right, he must have lost his balance, it wasn't a heart attack. Auntie Beaty has been coming round even more since then. She is always laughing and my father is always laughing, though not my mother. Sometimes Auntie Beaty is kind, gives me crisps and sherbet fountains, hugs me till I taste the perfume on her neck and lets me test how springy her black curls are. But other times Gillian and I say we're fed up playing with Josie, and my mother is sarcastic. Then my father gets cross and says we're all family and helping Beaty, and where's the harm?

I'm getting bored now in the back of the car, even though the roof's down, our hair in our faces. I'm in training for the Olympics, the hundred, the two hundred, the four hundred, the high jump, the long jump. At last year's village fête in our paddock, I came next to last in the under-nines dash, but I know I can do better this year. It was a bad day for other reasons. My mother had her terrible migraine, and maybe that affected my performance. I think it was my worst day ever – worse than when she skidded on the cow-muck and crashed the car; worse than when she ran screaming up the stairs because the wardrobe had fallen on top of Gillian; worse than when I was made to stay in bed all day as a punishment for still at my age dirtying my pants. I came back to the house after the tug-of-war and heard a noise from upstairs. She was moaning and rolling about on the bed, holding the back of her hand to her forehead. 'Get Daddy, quick,' she said, and I fetched him from the raffle, fast. I waited downstairs, then another doctor from the hospital came, and they told me to go back to the fête. At least I beat Christine Rawlinson in the race, but I should have beaten Stephen Ormrod as well. When I got back Lennie, the maid, said 'It's all right, she's at peace now,' and I thought she must mean: Your mummy's dead. She wasn't, and has had only two migraines since, but I worry that she might roll and moan with another strong one. In the Bible, when David is a boy, before meeting Goliath, he plays his harp at the court and the King's headaches disappear. I wish I could cure my mother's migraines like that, but I can only play the piano, and Mrs Brown says I need more practice before I can take Grade One. I think curing migraines is probably a much higher grade, Nine or Ten at least.

My father has turned off the lane on to a grass-seamed track between two gateposts. He parks the car, the hand-brake clicking tight, the silence after the ignition key. We are at the top of a hill, above a rough meadow with thistles and buttercups and cow parsley.

'Why don't you and Gill take Josephine down the hill,' he said. 'You'll be all right – just hold her hand. We can watch you from here.'

'Oh, Arthur, I'm not sure,' says Auntie Beaty.

'No, go on, they'll be fine,' he says. 'Lovely day, no sheep or cows to worry them, wonderful spot for children. Blake will look after her: he's nine now. Everything will be fine. Where's the harm?'

So we walk down the meadow, Josie's small hand trustingly in mine, which makes me feel big and in charge. I want to turn round to make sure my father and Auntie Beaty are watching us, but I don't. I'm not like Lot's wife in the picture at Sunday school. I'll show them I can be trusted.

On the level ground at the bottom of the field, there's nothing much to do, but I know we shouldn't turn back straight away. Gill begins to pick buttercups. Josie sits down on her terry-and-plastic bottom. She's too small to play games. I wish my father were here to sprint against. A lapwing wheels away from us, rising then plunging, and I think: 'Enough of your tricks. I know your nest is near. I could smash every egg if I tried.' I've learnt a lot about birds lately. We have a redstart's nest in the wall below the billiard-room. There was a pied wagtail on the lawn this morning, headbobbing and lifting its skirt, putting food in the mouth of its chick, which was fluffy and even bigger than its mother and should be fending for itself by now. And that distant cry just now was a curlew's, I think, getting faster and higher.

I look up the field to where the car's parked, but the windscreen is lit and flaring and I can't see behind it. It's as if all the power of the sun were in the glass containing Dad and Auntie Beaty, and no one else can look on it without being blinded. I put my hand – flat, as if saluting – over my eyes, and look again. I think I can see two heads there, close together, safe inside the blaze. I wait for the car doors to open, and I hear my father's voice again: 'Everything will be fine. Where's the harm?'

BINJAMIN WILKOMIRSKI

from *Fragments: Memories of a Childhood, 1939–48*

The first days in the orphanage were all confusion. There were so many new rules to learn, and most of them made no sense to me. Everything seemed to happen as endless contradictions.

The nurses were friendly, they didn't yell, they didn't hit us, they helped without being asked, and they brought clothes and food. Especially food!

It took your breath away. Every morning, mountains of unfamiliar luxuries were piled up on a sideboard, and there was enough for everyone – more than we all could eat.

On the other hand, I was always being forbidden to stick to the most important rules of survival. I had learned that stuff from Jankl in the big barracks, and I took such care not ever to forget any of it.

I knew that everything depended on it. But the nurses and the other children seemed to have forgotten it all. I often got the feeling that they'd never known the rules at all. They did everything with such dangerous carelessness.

Finally, nobody can know how long there'll be enough to eat. It can all come to an end any day. And maybe it's all just a trap, I said to myself.

I knew for sure that I had to be on the alert, because it was the clueless ones who always got into trouble first, and had the worst of it. Each meal could be the last for a long time. But nobody seemed to worry about this.

They always caught me stealing supplies, they always found my hiding places, they always saw through my plans to run away, and took their precautions. But oddly, they didn't punish me, at least not right away. And that was what was so unsettling. What were they planning?

Perhaps, I thought, they were holding off punishing me until they could catch me in a moment when I wasn't paying attention, and that would make it even worse.

I lived in a state of anxiety and watchfulness, all mixed up with breathless enjoyment of this temporary abundance.

But one thing in particular hurt me – I wasn't able to make any friends. I had always been friends with the ones like Jankl, who shared food with me.

Jankl used to steal food, when we were about to collapse from hunger. Jankl knew he'd be killed if he got caught. Jankl didn't eat what he'd stolen all himself, he gave me some, he always shared. Jankl was my friend.

But here, nobody wanted to share.

Once one of the older girls sat next to me at breakfast. She had the most beautiful eyes, and a soft voice. I held out half of my thick-buttered bread, but she just laughed at me and took her own piece of bread from the huge mound on the table.

As for the mound of bread on the table: an almost indescribable feeling went through me when I saw it that first morning after I arrived at the orphanage.

I was the last to arrive in the dining hall, because I didn't know that there would be food for us every morning. Only a few children were still sitting around the table.

I was shown where to sit. I sat down and waited. When no further signal came, I slowly looked up and glanced around cautiously – and there it was! Right in front of me on the table.

A big platter holding a mountain of bread. Clean-cut, even slices all beautifully stacked up in towers and turrets, and behind the towers, more, more than I could even count. I stared in awe, as if it were a holy relic.

Who could it belong to? I thought to myself. Who could be that powerful, and control so much bread? And why was it lying here unguarded? And would this person, whoever he was, give me a piece? Or should I try to steal one?

I looked at the bread and dilated my nostrils. A wonderful smell was coming in my direction, and suddenly I recognized this smell from before. But this time it was much stronger, and it enveloped me.

I remembered. It all came back in pictures which took me back to the day when I learned what the smell of bread was.

It was a day when the door to the barracks was opened. Bright light flowed in. My eyes still hurt.

'Binjamin! Is there a Binjamin here? Come out! Quick!' came a rough woman's voice from out of the light.

Hesitantly I stood up and went over, blinking, to the silhouette that stood in the open door. The dark outline told me that this was the same grey uniform that had brought me here from the farm. The same high boots, the same thick stockings, the same skirt hem that I had run alongside for so long.

'You're . . .?' I nodded.

'Today you can see your mother, but – only dahle.'

I didn't understand what she was saying. What did 'dahle' mean? I still have no idea today. She pronounced it with a very long, broad *aah*. And what did 'mother' mean?

I couldn't remember.

I had certainly heard other children using the word 'mother' from time to time. I'd heard some of them crying, and calling out for mama. And they fought about it.

Some of them said 'everyone has a mother.'

The others objected to this, and insisted that there were no mothers any more, that it had only been that way once, back then, a long time ago, in another world, before all the children had been brought together behind the fences and in the barracks. But since then there hadn't been any mothers, and the other world had disappeared long ago, forever. They said: 'There's no more world outside the fence!'

And I believed it.

They screamed at each other and called each other liars.

They began to strike out at each other bitterly.

All I understood was that a mother, whether you had one or not, must be something immensely important, something that was worth fighting for, the way you fought over food.

'Do you understand? You're going to see your mother! Do you understand?' the uniform lady said again.

I began to be afraid of her impatience. I shook my head and shrugged.

'You're going to come with me, and from now on you're not to talk. It is absolutely forbidden to say a single word, not now, not when you see your mother, not afterwards either. You won't ever talk about it to anyone ever, do you understand? Anyone, do you understand, do you?'

The last words came out almost in a shout. I shook my head and shrugged again.

Then she took home of my chin and pulled it up to make me look at her. All I could see was a shape and a blur that must be the peaked cap on her head. She bent down, stared into my eyes for a moment, and said in a clenched, soft voice:

'And if I so much as see you open your mouth, then I'll . . .'

And she made a terrible gesture over my head.

Now I nodded, and I knew she would kill me.

She took hold of my arm and dragged me off with her. I really didn't want to go. My knees were hurting, my eyes even more. I opened them briefly now and again, but the dazzling light burned and stabbed, and I could only see the path through a watery haze.

We walked and walked for ever, big gates in the fence were opened, then closed behind us again. At every gate she said something very quietly to the guards.

The brilliant reflection of the sun off the yellowish white sandy path burned in my eyes, and I was thirsty. My tongue felt like a lump, and my mouth was glued shut.

After a long time of miserable hurrying, stumbling, falling down, and hurrying on again, the woman suddenly stood still. I opened my eyes, she put her finger to her lips and looked at me severely. I nodded again. We were standing in front of a huge, dark barracks door. The sandy area in front of it glittered white in an ominous way.

Slowly and quietly she opened the door.

'All the way at the back, against the wall, on this side,' she said, pointing to the left.

She shut the door behind me quickly, without making a sound.

The dim light in the barracks felt good. I could make out a long central walkway, but there were no high wooden bunks down the two long sides: the walls were bare.

At first I thought the room was empty. But then I saw that there were people lying on the floor on covers over a bit of straw, on both sides of the walkway.

They seemed to be all women. They were hardly moving, and when they did, it was very, very slowly. I went carefully down between the bodies towards the wall.

At the foot of the last sleeping place, I came to a stop. I turned slowly toward the side that the uniform had pointed to.

I made out the shape of a body under a grey cover. The cover moved. A woman's head became visible, then two arms laying themselves slowly on top of the cover.

I bit my lips so as not to cry out. I looked unblinking into a face that looked back at me with huge eyes.

Was this my mother, my dahle?

One of the children had once said that if you have mother, she belongs just to you! So this woman belonged to me, just me? I wondered.

But I wasn't allowed to ask. I wanted to tell her that I wasn't allowed to speak, that they'd kill me if I said anything to her – but I couldn't do that.

So I stood there in silence, clenching my teeth together, and didn't dare move. I didn't look away from her once. For just a moment the face seemed to smile, but I couldn't be sure.

I don't know how long I stood there like that. A loud creak broke the silence, the door opened a crack – the sign that time was up. At that moment, the woman moved one of her arms, groping with her hand under the straw and the lumps between her and the wall, as if she was looking for something. The hand re-emerged, clutching something. She motioned for me to come closer.

I kept standing there without moving. I was waiting, I was afraid. She beckoned faster, more urgently. Slowly I fought down my shyness. I went up to her.

Now I could see the face more clearly, it was shiny and wet, and I saw that it was crying. Without saying a word she reached out her hand to me and indicated that I should take what she had brought out from under the straw. For a single moment I touched her hand – it felt hot and damp.

I took the object, clutched it tight against me, and went towards the door, which now stood wide open, silhouetting the dark waiting shape of the grey uniform skirt and the peaked cap.

We went back the way we'd come. The woman held my arm, dragging me along behind her. I used my free hand to grope the unknown object with curiosity. It had jagged edges and corners, and felt coarse and hard.

'What is this?' I asked the grey uniform as we reached my barracks.

'That's bread,' she said, and 'You have to soften it in water, then you can eat it.' Then she went away.

I spent a long time chewing on the softened bread and then dunking it again into the little ration of water in my mug, and chewing again, over and over again, until the water was all used up and the crust had shrunk to a tiny little ball.

Finally all that remained was the indescribably delicious smell of bread on my fingers as I held them to my nose again and again.

I only ever saw the lady in the grey uniform once again. I recognized her by the rhythm of her stride. She was hurrying somewhere and I ran up to her. I thought she would look for me and take me to my mother. She stood still for just a moment and looked at me. It took her a second to recognize me.

'Oh, it's you . . . you can't see your mother again . . . it's not possible any more.'

She hurried off without a further thought.

I observed the other children. They were taking some kind of thick red stuff out of a jar and putting it on their bread before they ate it.

I didn't dare take a slice from the bread pile in front of everyone. So I picked up my spoon and went over to the jar with the red stuff. I dipped the spoon in and licked it off.

It tasted so sweet! I tried it again. But a smack on my hand stopped me. A white apron bent over me.

'You're not allowed to do that. Only with bread!' she said severely.

'But the bread doesn't belong to me,' I said. My eyes began to smart, I felt tears coming and I was ashamed.

'Here's a piece of bread for you and now you can . . .' was all she had time to say.

'I only take bread from my mother,' I screamed at her in tears of fury, and ran from the room.

But where to? I didn't know the building. The nurse followed me and took me by the shoulders. I wondered whether to bite her or not, but the situation seemed hopeless, so I clutched one arm over my stomach to protect it and held the other over my head and waited for the blows, but nothing happened. I took a quick look up at her – and saw that she was smiling.

So I let myself be led back to the table, but I didn't drop my guard. She took another piece of bread from the mound and used a knife to smear it with a thick layer of the good sweet stuff.

'This is my present to you,' she said.

I was hungry, and hesitantly I began to eat.

WALTER DE LA MARE

'Keep Innocency'

Like an old battle, youth is wild
With bugle and spear, and counter cry,
Fanfare and drummery, yet a child
Dreaming of that sweet chivalry,
The piercing terror cannot see.

He, with a mild and serious eye,
Along the azure of the years,
Sees the sweet pomp sweep hurtling by;
But he sees not death's blood and tears,
Sees not the plunging of the spears.

And all the strident horror of
Horse and rider, in red defeat,
Is only music fine enough
To lull him into slumber sweet
In fields where ewe and lambkin bleat.

O, if with such simplicity
Himself take arms and suffer war;
With beams his targe shall gilded be,
Though in the thickening gloom be far
The steadfast light of any star!

Though hoarse War's eagle on him perch,
Quickened with guilty lightnings – there
It shall in vain for terror search,
Where a child's eyes 'neath bloody hair
Gaze purely through the dingy air.

And when the wheeling rout is spent,
Though in the heaps of slain he lie;
Or lonely in his last content;
Quenchless shall burn in secrecy
The flame Death knows his victors by.

CHARLES DICKENS

from *Oliver Twist*

Oliver had not been within the walls of the workhouse a quarter of an hour, and had scarcely completed the demolition of a second slice of bread, when Mr Bumble, who had handed him over to the care of an old woman, returned; and, telling him it was a board night, informed him that the board had said he was to appear before it forthwith.

Not having a very clearly defined notion of what a live board was, Oliver was rather astounded by this intelligence, and was not quite certain whether he ought to laugh or cry. He had no time to think about the matter, however; for Mr Bumble gave him a tap on the head, with his cane, to wake him up; and another on the back to make him lively; and bidding him follow, conducted him into a large whitewashed room, where eight or ten fat gentlemen were sitting round a table. At the top of the table, seated in an armchair rather higher than the rest, was a particularly fat gentleman with a very round, red face.

'Bow to the board,' said Bumble. Oliver brushed away two or three tears that were lingering in his eyes; and seeing no board but the table, fortunately bowed to that.

'What's your name, boy?' said the gentleman in the high chair.

Oliver was frightened at the sight of so many gentlemen, which made him tremble; but the beadle gave him another tap behind, which made him cry. These two causes made him answer in a very low and hesitating voice; whereupon a gentleman in a white waistcoat said he was a fool. Which was a capital way of raising his spirits, and putting him quite at his ease.

'Boy,' said the gentleman in the high chair, 'listen to me. You know you're an orphan, I suppose?'

'What's that, sir?' inquired poor Oliver.

'The boy *is* a fool – I thought he was,' said the gentleman in the white waistcoat.

'Hush!' said the gentleman who had spoken first. 'You know you've got no father or mother, and that you were brought up by the parish, don't you?'

'Yes, sir,' replied Oliver, weeping bitterly.

'What are you crying for?' inquired the gentleman in the white waistcoat. And to be sure it was very extraordinary. What *could* the boy be crying for?

'I hope you say your prayers every night,' said another gentleman in a gruff voice; 'and pray for the people who feed you, and take care of you – like a Christian.'

'Yes, sir,' stammered the boy. The gentleman who spoke last was unconsciously right. It would have been *very* like a Christian, and a marvellously good Christian, too, if Oliver had prayed for the people who fed and took care of *him*. But he hadn't, because nobody had taught him.

'Well! You have come here to be educated, and taught a useful trade,' said the red-faced gentleman in the high chair.

'So you'll begin to pick oakum tomorrow morning at six o'clock,' added the surly one in the white waistcoat.

For the combination of both these blessings in the one simple process of picking oakum, Oliver bowed low by the direction of the beadle, and was then hurried away to a large ward: where, on a rough, hard bed, he sobbed himself to sleep. What a noble illustration of the tender laws of England! They let the paupers go to sleep!

Poor Oliver! He little thought, as he lay sleeping in happy unconsciousness of all around him, that the board had that very day arrived at a decision which would exercise the most material influence over all his future fortunes. But they had. And this was it:

The members of this board were very sage, deep, philosophical men; and when they came to turn their attention to the workhouse, they found out at once, what ordinary folks would never have discovered – the poor people liked it! It was a regular place of public entertainment for the poorer classes; a tavern where there was nothing to pay; a public breakfast, dinner, tea and supper all the year round; a brick and mortar elysium, where it was all play and no work. 'Oho!' said the board, looking very knowing; 'we are the fellows to set this to rights; we'll stop it all, in no time.' So, they established the rule, that all poor people should have the alternative (for they would compel nobody, not they), of being starved by a gradual process in the house, or by a quick one out of it. With this view, they contracted with the water-works to lay on an unlimited supply of water; and with a corn-factor to supply periodically small quantities of oatmeal; and issued three meals of thin gruel a day, with an onion twice a week, and half a roll on Sundays. They made a great many other wise and humane regulations, having reference to the ladies, which it is not necessary to repeat; kindly undertook to divorce poor married people, in consequence of the great expense of a suit in Doctors' Commons; and, instead of compelling a man to support his family, as they had theretofore done, took his family away from him, and made him a bachelor! There is no saying how many applicants for relief, under these last two heads, might have started up in all classes of society, if it had not been coupled with the workhouse; but the board were long-headed men, and had provided for this difficulty. The relief was inseparable from the workhouse and the gruel; and that frightened people.

For the first six months after Oliver Twist was removed, the system was in full operation. It was rather expensive at first, in consequence of the increase in the undertaker's bill, and the necessity of taking in the clothes of all the paupers, which fluttered loosely on their wasted, shrunken forms, after a week or two's gruel. But the number of workhouse inmates got thin as well as the paupers; and the board were in ecstasies.

The room in which the boys were fed, was a large stone hall, with a copper at one end; out of which the master, dressed in an apron for the purpose, and assisted by one or two women, ladled the gruel at mealtimes. Of this festive composition each boy had one porringer, and no more – except on occasions of great public rejoicing, when he had two ounces and a quarter of bread besides. The bowls never wanted washing. The boys polished them with their spoons till they shone again; and when they had performed this operation (which never took very long, the spoons being nearly as large as the bowls), they would sit staring at the copper, with such eager eyes, as if they could have devoured the very bricks of which it was composed; employing themselves, meanwhile, in sucking their fingers most assiduously, with the view of catching up any stray splashes of gruel that might have been cast thereon. Boys have generally excellent appetites. Oliver Twist and his companions suffered the tortures of slow starvation for three months: at last they got so voracious and wild with hunger, that one boy, who was tall for his age, and hadn't been used to that sort of thing (for his father had kept a small cook-shop), hinted darkly to his companions, that unless he had another basin of gruel *per diem*, he was afraid he might some night happen to eat the boy who slept next him, who happened to be a weakly youth of tender age. He had a wild, hungry eye; and they implicitly believed him. A council was held; lots were cast who should walk up to the master after supper that evening, and ask for more; and it fell to Oliver Twist.

The evening arrived; the boys took their places. The master, in his cook's uniform, stationed himself at the copper; his pauper assistants ranged themselves behind him; the gruel was served out; and a long grace was said over the short commons. The gruel disappeared; the boys whispered each other, and winked at Oliver; while his next neighbours nudged him. Child as he was, he was desperate with hunger, and reckless with misery. He rose from the table; and advancing to the master, basin and spoon in hand, said: somewhat alarmed at his own temerity:

'Please, sir, I want so more.'

The master was a fat, healthy man; but he turned very pale. He gazed in stupefied astonishment on the small rebel for some seconds, and then clung for support to the copper. The assistants were paralysed with wonder; the boys with fear.

'What!' said the master at length, in a faint voice.

'Please, sir,' replied Oliver, 'I want some more.'

The master aimed a blow at Oliver's head with the ladle; pinioned him in his arms; and shrieked aloud for the beadle.

The board were sitting in solemn conclave, when Mr Bumble rushed into the room in great excitement, and addressing the gentleman in the high chair, said,

'Mr Limbkins, I beg your pardon, sir! Oliver Twist has asked for more!'

There was a general start. Horror was depicted on every countenance.

'For *more!*' said Mr Limbkins. 'Compose yourself, Bumble, and answer me distinctly. Do I understand that he asked for more, after he had eaten the supper allotted by the dietary?'

'He did, sir,' replied Bumble.

'That boy will be hung,' said the gentleman in the white waistcoat. 'I know that boy will be hung.'

Nobody controverted the prophetic gentleman's opinion. An animated discussion took place. Oliver was ordered into instant confinement; and a bill was next morning pasted on the outside of the gate, offering a reward of five pounds to anybody who would take Oliver Twist off the hands of the parish. In other words, five pounds and Oliver Twist were offered to any man or woman who wanted an apprentice to any trade, business or calling.

'I never was more convinced of anything in my life,' said the gentleman in the white waistcoat, as he knocked at the gate and read the bill next morning: 'I never was more convinced of anything in my life, than I am that that boy will come to be hung.'

As I purpose to show in the sequel whether the white waistcoated gentleman was right or not, I should perhaps mar the interest of this narrative (supposing it to possess any at all), if I ventured to hint just yet, whether the life of Oliver Twist had this violent termination or no.

PAMELA GLENCONNER

from *The Sayings of the Children* (1918)

'What is a wife?' asked One, after a thoughtful pause.
'I am wife to Daddy.'
'And is Daddy your wife?'
'No, Daddy is my husband.'
'Then who are you?'

SAKI

'The Lumber-Room'

The children were to be driven, as a special treat, to the sands at Jagborough. Nicholas was not to be one of the party; he was in disgrace. Only that morning he had refused to eat his wholesome bread and milk on the seemingly frivolous ground that there was a frog in it. Older and wiser and better people had told him that there could not possibly be a frog in his bread and milk and that he was not to talk nonsense; he continued, nevertheless, to talk what seemed the veriest nonsense, and described with much detail the colouration and markings of the alleged frog. The dramatic part of the incident was that there really was a frog in Nicholas's basin of bread and milk; he had put it there himself, so he felt entitled to know something about it. The sin of taking a frog from the garden and putting it into a bowl of wholesome bread and milk was enlarged on at great length, but the fact that stood out clearest in the whole affair, as it presented itself to the mind of Nicholas, was that the older, wiser and better people had been proved to be profoundly in error in matters about which they had expressed the utmost assurance.

'You said there couldn't possibly be a frog in my bread and milk; there *was* a frog in my bread and milk,' he repeated, with the insistence of a skilled tactician who does not intend to shift from favourable ground.

So his boy-cousin and girl-cousin and his quite uninteresting younger brother were to be taken to Jagborough sands that afternoon and he was to stay at home. His cousins' aunt, who insisted, by an unwarranted stretch of imagination, in styling herself his aunt also, had hastily invented the Jagborough expedition in order to impress on Nicholas the delights that he had justly forfeited by his disgraceful conduct at the breakfast table. It was her habit, whenever one of the children fell from grace, to improvise something of a festival nature from which the offender would be rigorously debarred; if all the children sinned collectively they were suddenly informed of a circus in the neighbouring town, a circus of unrivalled merit and uncounted elephants, to which, but for their depravity, they would have been taken that very day.

A few decent tears were looked for on the part of Nicholas when the moment for the departure of the expedition arrived. As a matter of fact, however, all the crying was done by his girl-cousin, who scraped her knee rather painfully against the step of the carriage as she was scrambling in.

'How she did howl,' said Nicholas cheerfully, as the party drove off without any of the elation of high spirits that should have characterized it.

'She'll soon get over that,' said the *soi-disant* aunt; 'it will be a glorious afternoon for racing about over those beautiful sands. How they will enjoy themselves!'

'Bobby won't enjoy himself much, and he won't race much either,' said Nicholas with a grim chuckle; 'his boots are hurting him. They're too tight.'

'Why didn't he tell me they were hurting?' asked the aunt with some asperity.

'He told you twice, but you weren't listening. You often don't listen when we tell you important things.'

'You are not to go into the gooseberry garden,' said the aunt, changing the subject.

'Why not?' demanded Nicholas.

'Because you are in disgrace,' said the aunt loftily.

Nicholas did not admit the flawlessness of the reasoning; he felt perfectly capable of being in disgrace and in a gooseberry garden at the same moment. His face took on an expression of considerable obstinacy. It was clear to his aunt that he was determined to get into the gooseberry garden, 'only,' as she remarked to herself, 'because I have told him he is not to.'

Now the gooseberry garden had two doors by which it might be entered, and once a small person like Nicholas could slip in there he could effectually disappear from view amid the masking growth of artichokes, raspberry canes and fruit bushes. The aunt had many other things to do that afternoon, but she spent an hour or two in trivial gardening operations among flower beds and shrubberies, whence she could keep a watchful eye on the two doors that led to the forbidden paradise. She was a woman of few ideas, with immense powers of concentration.

Nicholas made one or two sorties into the front garden, wriggling his way with obvious stealth of purpose towards one or other of the doors, but never able for a moment to evade the aunt's watchful eye. As a matter of fact, he had no intention of trying to get into the gooseberry garden, but it was extremely convenient for him that his aunt should believe that he had; it was a belief that would keep her on self-imposed sentry-duty for the greater part of the afternoon. Having thoroughly confimed and fortified her suspicions, Nicholas slipped back into the house and rapidly put into execution a plan of action that had long germinated in his brain. By standing on a chair in the library one could reach a shelf on which reposed a fat, important-looking key. The key was as important as it looked; it was the instrument which kept the mysteries of the lumber-room secure from unauthorized intrusion, which opened a way only for aunts and such-like privileged persons. Nicholas had not had much experience of the art of fitting keys into keyholes and turning locks, but for some days past he had practised with the key of the schoolroom door; he did not believe in trusting too much to luck and accident. The key turned stiffly in the lock, but it turned. The door opened, and Nicholas was in an unknown land, compared with which the gooseberry garden was a stale delight, a mere material pleasure.

Often and often Nicholas had pictured to himself what the lumber-room might be like, that region that was so carefully sealed from youthful eyes and concerning which no questions were ever answered. It came up to his expectations. In the first place it was large and dimly lit, one high window opening on to the forbidden garden being its only source of illumination. In the second place it was a storehouse of unimagined treasures. The aunt-by-assertion was one of those people who think that things spoil by use and consign them to dust and damp by way of preserving them. Such parts of the house as Nicholas knew best were rather bare and cheerless, but here there were wonderful things for the eye to feast on. First and foremost there was a piece of framed tapestry that was evidently meant to be a fire-screen. To Nicholas it was a living, breathing story; he sat down on a roll of Indian hangings, glowing in wonderful colours beneath a layer of dust, and took in all the details of the tapestry picture. A man, dressed in the hunting costume of some remote period, had just transfixed a stag with an arrow; it could not have been a difficult shot because the stag was only one or two paces away from him; in the thickly growing vegetation that the picture suggested it would not have been difficult to creep up to a feeding stag, and the two spotted dogs that were springing forward to join in the chase had evidently been trained to keep to heel till the arrow was discharged. That part of the picture was simple, if interesting, but did the huntsman see, what Nicholas saw, that four galloping wolves were coming in his direction through the wood? There might be more than four of them hidden behind the trees, and in any case would the man and his dogs be able to cope with the four wolves if they made an attack? The man had only two arrows left in his quiver, and he might miss with one or both of them; all one knew about his skill in shooting was that he could hit a large stag at a ridiculously short range. Nicholas sat for many golden minutes revolving the possibilities of the scene; he was inclined to think that there were more than four wolves and that the man and his dogs were in a tight corner.

But there were other objects of delight and interest claiming his instant attention; there were quaint twisted candlesticks in the shape of snakes, and a teapot fashioned like a china duck, out of whose open beak the tea was supposed to come. How dull and shapeless the nursery teapot seemed in comparison! And there was a carved sandalwood box packed tight with aromatic cotton-wool, and between the layers of cotton-wool were little brass figures, hump-necked bulls, and peacocks and goblins, delightful to see and to handle. Less promising in appearance was a large square book with plain black covers; Nicholas peeped into it, and, behold, it was full of coloured pictures of birds. And such birds! In the garden, and in the lanes when he went for a walk, Nicholas came across a few birds, of which the largest were an occasional magpie or wood pigeon; here were herons and bustards, kites, toucans, tiger-bitterns, brush turkeys, ibises, golden pheasants, a whole portrait gallery of undreamed-of creatures. And as he was admiring the colouring of the mandarin duck and assigning a life history to it, the voice of his aunt in shrill vociferation of his name came from the gooseberry garden without. She had grown suspicious at his long disappearance, and had leapt to the conclusion that he had climbed over the wall behind the sheltering screen of the lilac bushes; she was now engaged in energetic and rather hopeless search for him among the artichokes and raspberry canes.

'Nicholas, Nicholas!' she screamed, 'you are to come out of this at once. It's no use trying to hide there; I can see you all the time.'

It was probably the first time for twenty years that anyone had smiled in that lumber-room.

Presently the angry repetitions of Nicholas's name gave way to a shriek, and a cry for somebody to come quickly, Nicholas shut the book, restored it carefully to its place in a corner, and shook some dust from a neighbouring pile of newspapers over it. Then he crept from the room, locked the door, and replaced the key exactly where he had found it. His aunt was still calling his name when he sauntered into the front garden.

'Who's calling?' he asked.

'Me,' came the answer from the other side of the wall; 'didn't you hear me? I've been looking for you in the gooseberry garden, and I've slipped into the rain-water tank. Luckily there's no water in it, but the sides are slippery and I can't get out. Fetch the little ladder from under the cherry tree—'

'I was told I wasn't to go into the gooseberry garden,' said Nicholas promptly.

'I told you not to, and now I tell you that you may,' came the voice from the rain-water tank, rather impatiently.

'Your voice doesn't sound like aunt's,' objected Nicholas; 'you may be the Evil One tempting me to be disobedient. Aunt often tells me that the Evil One tempts me and that I always yield. This time I'm not going to yield.'

'Don't talk nonsense,' said the prisoner in the tank; 'go and fetch the ladder.'

'Will there be strawberry jam for tea?' asked Nicholas innocently.

'Certainly there will be,' said the aunt, privately resolving that Nicholas should have none of it.

'Now I know that you are the Evil One and not aunt,' shouted Nicholas gleefully; 'when we asked aunt for strawberry jam yesterday she said there wasn't any. I know there are four jars of it in the store cupboard, because I looked, and of course you know it's there, but *she* doesn't, because she said there wasn't any. Oh, Devil, you *have* sold yourself!'

There was an unusual sense of luxury in being able to talk to an aunt as though one was talking to the Evil One, but Nicholas knew, with childish discernment, that such luxuries were not to be over-indulged in. He walked noisily away, and it was a kitchen-maid, in search of parsley, who eventually rescued the aunt from the rain-water tank.

Tea that evening was partaken of in a fearsome silence. The tide had been at its highest when the children had arrived at Jagborough Cove, so there had been no sands to play on – a circumstance that the aunt had overlooked in the haste of organizing her punitive expedition. The tightness of Bobby's boots had had disastrous effect on his temper the whole of the afternoon, and altogether the children could not have been said to have enjoyed themselves. The aunt maintained the frozen muteness of one who has suffered undignified and unmerited detention in a rain-water tank for thirty-five minutes. As for Nicholas, he, too, was silent, in the absorption of one who has much to think about; it was just possible, he considered, that the huntsman would escape with his hounds while the wolves feasted on the stricken stag.

HILAIRE BELLOC

'Jim, Who Ran Away From His Nurse, and Was Eaten By a Lion'

There was a Boy whose name was Jim;
His Friends were very good to him.
They gave him Tea, and Cakes, and Jam,
And slices of delicious Ham,
And Chocolate with pink inside,
And little Tricycles to ride,
And read him Stories through and through,
And even took him to the Zoo –
But there it was the dreadful Fate
Befell him, which I now relate.

You know – at least you ought to know,
For I have often told you so –
That Children never are allowed
To leave their Nurses in a Crowd;
Now this was Jim's especial Foible,
He ran away when he was able,
And on this inauspicious day
He slipped his hand and ran away!
He hadn't gone a yard when – Bang!
With open Jaws, a Lion sprang,
And hungrily began to eat
The Boy: beginning at his feet.

Now, just imagine how it feels
When first your toes and then your heels,
And then by gradual degrees,
Your shins and ankles, calves and knees,
Are slowly eaten, bit by bit.
No wonder Jim detested it!
No wonder that he shouted 'Hi!'
The Honest Keeper heard his cry,
Though very fat he almost ran
To help the little gentleman.
'Ponto!' he ordered as he came
(For Ponto was the Lion's name),
'Ponto!' he cried, with angry Frown.
'Let go, Sir! Down, Sir! Put it down!'

The Lion made a sudden Stop,
He let the Dainty Morsel drop,
And slunk reluctant to his Cage,
Snarling with Disappointed Rage.
But when he bent him over Jim,
The Honest Keeper's Eyes were dim.
The Lion having reached his Head,
The Miserable Boy was dead!
When Nurse informed his Parents, they
Were more Concerned than I can say:–
His Mother, as she dried her eyes,
Said, 'Well – it gives me no surprise,
He would not do as he was told!'
His Father, who was self-controlled,
Bade all the children round attend
To James' miserable end,
And always keep a-hold of Nurse
For fear of finding something worse.

SAMUEL BUTLER

from *The Way of All Flesh*

In the course of the evening they came into the drawing-room and as an especial treat were to sing some of their hymns to me instead of saying them, so that I might hear how nicely they sang. Ernest was to choose the first hymn and he chose one about some people who were to come to the sunset tree. I am no botanist, and do not know what kind of a tree a sunset tree is, but the words began, 'Come, come, come; come to the sunset tree for the day is past and gone.' The tune was rather pretty and had taken Ernest's fancy, for he was unusually fond of music and had a sweet little child's voice which he liked using. He was, however, very late in being about to sound a hard C or K, and instead of saying 'Come,' he said 'tum, tum, tum'.

'Ernest,' said Theobald from the armchair in front of the fire where he was sitting with his hands folded before him, 'don't you think it would be very nice if you were to say "come" like other people, instead of "tum"?'

'I do say tum,' replied Ernest, meaning that he had said 'come'.

Theobald was always in a bad temper on Sunday evening. Whether it is that they are as much bored with their day as their neighbour, or whether they are tired, or whatever the cause may be, clergymen are seldom at their best on Sunday evening; I had already seen signs that evening that my host was cross, and was a little nervous at hearing Ernest say so promptly, 'I do say tum,' when his papa had said he did not say it as he should.

Theobald noticed the fact that he was being contradicted in a moment. He had been sitting in an armchair in front of the fire with his hands folded, doing nothing, but he got up at once and went to the piano.

'No Ernest, you don't,' he said; 'you say nothing of the kind, you say "tum" not "come". Now say "come" after me, as I do.'

'Tum,' said Ernest at once. 'Is that better?' I have no doubt he thought it was, but it was not.

'Now Ernest, you are not taking pains: you are not trying as you ought to do. It is high time you learned to say "come"; why Joey can say "come", can't you, Joey?'

'Yeth I can,' replied Joey promptly, and he said something which was not far off 'come'.

'There, Ernest, do you hear that? There's no difficulty about it now, no shadow of difficulty. Now take your own time; think about it and say "come" after me.'

The boy remained silent for a few seconds and then said 'tum' again.

I laughed, but Theobald turned to me impatiently and said, 'Please do not laugh Overton, it will make the boy think it does not matter, and it matters a great deal'; then turning to Ernest he said, 'Now Ernest, I will give you one more chance, and if you don't say "come" I shall know that you are self-willed and naughty.'

He looked very angry and a shade came over Ernest's face, like that which comes upon the face of a puppy when it is being scolded without understanding why. The child saw well what was coming now, was frightened, and of course said 'tum' once more.

'Very well Ernest,' said his father, catching him angrily by the shoulder. 'I have done my best to save you but if you will have it so you will,' and he lugged the little wretch out of the room crying by anticipation. A few minutes more and we could hear screams coming from the dining-room across the hall which separated the drawing-room from the dining-room, and knew that poor Ernest was being beaten. 'I have sent him to bed,' said Theobald, as he returned to the drawing-room, 'and now, Christina, I think we will have the servants in to prayers,' and he rang the bell for them, red-handed as he was.

ANONYMOUS

'Mother may I go and Bathe?'

Mother may I go and Bathe?
Yes, my darling daughter.
Hang your clothes on yonder tree
But don't go near the water.

ELSPETH BARKER

from *O Caledonia*

One afternoon she was told to bring the baby in from the garden. Reluctantly she trailed out into the still early autumn air. The pram was on the lawn some way from the house. With clumsy fingers Janet undid the stiff navy cover, pulled back innumerable blankets and scrabbled under the hood for the swaddled occupant, who began to roar, fixing Janet with an unblinking glare. It was difficult to pull her from under the hood; Janet tried to lower it and cut her finger in its joint so that blood dripped on to the baby's shawls. Louder came the roars. It began to rain. The shawls were unravelling and catching on the metal parts of the hood; she pulled at them and tore a great hole in the lacy cobweb. In desperation Janet seized the infant by her head and dragged her out, clutching at corners of shawl and looping them over the flailing torso. The whole bundle slithered through her hands and lay shrieking frantically on the dank grass. Janet could not lift it up; it was far heavier than she would ever have guessed; when she had held the baby before, she had simply been deposited on her lap; she had never carried her. So she grabbed such projections as she could find, a shoulder and a fiercely resisting arm, and dragged the whole mass, shawls trailing, through mud and snagging on leaves, over the grass and across the gravel and at last to the kitchen door where Vera and Nanny greeted her, first with horror and then with fury.

'What in the world have you been doing? What have you done? Where's the pram? You were told to bring the baby in, in the *pram* of course. You've no business to try to carry her. How dare you?' Not one word of Janet's explanations did they hear. Once again it was spanking and disgrace and a distant overheard muttering of '... simply can't be trusted', 'We should have known better', 'After what she did before', 'Keep her away from the little ones'. Good. But then, 'Best not to tell her grandfather, it'll break his heart.' A BROKEN HEART. Nanny's sister had died of a broken heart. She crept away to the glory-hole under the stairs and sat howling in an abyss of guilt among the boxes of candles and dusty jars of lentils and syrupy bottled gooseberries and raspberries, until she could howl no more. Then she went to the nursery and lay on the floor and read stories of princesses with broken hearts. She was bad and she knew she was bad and she could see no end to it.

ADRIAN HENRI

'Beatrix is Three'

At the top of the stairs
I ask for her hand. O.K.
She gives it to me.
How her fist fits my palm,
A bunch of consolation.
We take our time
Down the steep carpetway
As I wish silently
That the stairs were endless.

LIZ LOCHHEAD

'Everybody's Mother'

Of course
everybody's mother always and
so on . . .

Always never
loved you enough
or too smothering much.

Of course you were the Only One, your
mother
a machine
that shat out siblings, listen

everybody's mother
was the original Frigid-
aire Icequeen clunking out
the hardstuff in nuggets, mirror-
silvers and ice-splinters that'd stick
in your heart.

Absolutely everyone's mother
was artistic when she was young.

Everyone's mother
was a perfumed presence with pearls, remote

white shoulders when she
bent over in her ball dress
to kiss you in your crib.

Everybody's mother slept with the butcher
for sausages to stuff you with.

Everyone's mother
mythologized herself. You got mixed up
between dragon's teeth and blackmarket stockings.

Naturally
she failed to give you
Positive Feelings
about your own sorry
sprouting body (it was a bloody shame)

but she did
sit up all night sewing sequins
on your carnival costume

so you would have a good time

and she spat
on the corner of her hanky and scraped
at your mouth with sour lace till you squirmed

so you would look smart

And where
was your father all this time?
Away
at the war, or
in his office, or any-
way conspicuous for his
Absence, so

what if your mother did
float around above you
big as a barrage balloon
blocking out the light?

Nobody's mother can't not never do nothing right.

GEORGE ELIOT

from *The Mill on the Floss*

It was a heavy disappointment to Maggie that she was not allowed to go with her father in the gig when he went to fetch Tom home from the Academy; but the morning was too wet, Mrs Tulliver said, for a little girl to go out in her best bonnet. Maggie took the opposite view very strongly, and it was a direct consequence of this difference of opinion that when her mother was in the act of brushing out the reluctant black crop, Maggie suddenly rushed from under her hands and dipped her head in a basin of water standing near – in the vindictive determination that there should be no more chance of curls that day.

'Maggie, Maggie,' exclaimed Mrs Tulliver, sitting stout and helpless with the brushes on her lap, 'what is to become of you, if you're so naughty? I'll tell your aunt Glegg and your aunt Pullet when they come next week, and they'll never love you any more. Oh dear, Oh dear, look at your clean pinafore, wet from top to bottom. Folks'll think it's a judgment on me as I've got such a child – they'll think I've done summat wicked.'

Before this remonstrance was finished Maggie was already out of hearing, making her way towards the great attic that ran under the old high-pitched roof, shaking the water from her black locks as she ran, like a Skye terrier escaped from his bath. This attic was Maggie's favourite retreat on a wet day, when the weather was not too cold:

here she fretted out all her ill-humours, and talked aloud to the worm-eaten floors and the worm-eaten shelves and the dark rafters festooned with cobwebs, and here she kept a fetish which she punished for all her misfortunes. This was the trunk of a large wooden doll, which once stared with the roundest of eyes above the reddest of cheeks, but was now entirely defaced by a long career of vicarious suffering. Three nails driven into the head commemorated as many crises in Maggie's nine years of earthly struggle; that luxury of vengeance having been suggested to her by the picture of Jael destroying Sisera in the old Bible. The last nail had been driven in with a fiercer stroke than usual, for the fetish on that occasion represented aunt Glegg. But immediately afterwards Maggie had reflected that if she drove many nails in, she would not be so well able to fancy that the head was hurt when she knocked it against the wall, nor to comfort it, and make believe to poultice it when her fury was abated; for even aunt Glegg would be pitiable when she had been hurt very much, and thoroughly humiliated, so as to beg her niece's pardon. Since then, she had driven no more nails in, but had soothed herself by alternately grinding and beating the wooden head against the rough brick of the great chimneys that made two square pillars supporting the roof. That was what she did this morning on reaching the attic, sobbing all the while with a passion that expelled every other form of consciousness – even the memory of the grievance that had caused it. As at last the sobs were getting quieter and the grinding less fierce, a sudden beam of sunshine, falling through the wire lattice across the worm-eaten shelves, made her throw away the fetish and run to the window. The sun was really breaking out, the sound of the mill seemed cheerful again, the granary doors were open, and there was Yap, the queer white and brown terrier with one ear turned back, trotting about and sniffing vaguely as if he were in search of a companion. It was irresistible: Maggie tossed her hair back and ran downstairs, seized her bonnet without putting it on, peeped and then dashed along the passage lest she should encounter her mother, and was quickly out in the yard, whirling round like a Pythoness and singing as she whirled, 'Yap, Yap, Tom's coming home', while Yap pranced and barked round her, as much as to say, if there was any noise wanted, he was the dog for it.

'Hegh, hegh, Miss, you'll make yourself giddy an' tumble down i' the dirt,' said Luke, the head miller, a tall broad-shouldered man of forty, black-eyed and black-haired, subdued by a general mealiness, like an auricula.

Maggie paused in her whirling and said, staggering a little, 'Oh no, it doesn't make me giddy. Luke, may I go into the mill with you?'

Maggie loved to linger in the great spaces of the mill, and often came out with her black hair powdered to a soft whiteness that made her dark eyes flash out with new fire. The resolute din, the unresting motion of the great stones giving her a dim delicious awe as at the presence of an uncontrollable force, the meal for ever pouring, pouring, the fine white powder softening all surfaces and making the very spider-nets look like faery lacework, the sweet pure scent of the meal – all helped to make Maggie feel that the mill was a little world apart from her outside everyday life. The spiders were especially a subject of speculation with her: she wondered if they had any relations outside the mill, for in that case there must be a painful difficulty in their family intercourse: a fat and floury spider, accustomed to take his fly well dusted with meal, must suffer a little at a cousin's table where the fly was *au naturel*, and the lady spiders must be mutually shocked at each other's appearance. But the part of the mill she liked best was the topmost story – the corn-hutch where there were the great heaps of grain which she could sit on and slide down continually. She was in the habit of taking this recreation as she conversed with Luke, to whom she was very communicative, wishing him to think well of her understanding, as her father did.

Perhaps she felt it necessary to recover her position with him on the present occasion, for, as she sat sliding on the heap of grain near which he was busying himself, she said, at that shrill pitch which was requisite in mill-society:

'I think you never read any book but the Bible, did you, Luke?'

'Nay, Miss – an' not much o' that,' said Luke, with great frankness. 'I'm no reader, I arn't.'

'But if I lent you one of my books, Luke? I've not got any *very* pretty books that would be easy for you to read; but there's *Pug's Tour of Europe* – that would tell you all about the different sorts of people in the world, and if you didn't understand the reading, the pictures would help you – they show the looks and ways of the people and what they do. There are Dutchmen, very fat, and smoking, you know – and one sitting on a barrel.'

'Nay, Miss, I'n no opinion o' Dutchmen. There ben't much good i' knowin' about *them*.'

'But they're our fellow-creatures, Luke – we ought to know about our fellow creatures.'

'Not much o' fellow creaturs, I think, Miss: all I know – my old master, as war a knowin' man, used to say, says he, "If e'er I sow my wheat wi'out brinin', I'm a Dutchman," says he; an' that war as much as to say as a Dutchman war a fool, or next door. Nay, nay, I arn't goin' to bother mysen about Dutchmen. There's fools enoo – an' rogues enoo – wi'out lookin' i' books for 'em.'

'Oh well,' said Maggie, rather foiled by Luke's unexpectedly decided views about Dutchmen, 'Perhaps you would like *Animated Nature* better – that's not Dutchmen, you know, but elephants, and kangaroos, and the civet cat, and the sun-fish, and a bird sitting on its tail – I forget its name. There are countries full of those creatures, instead of horses and cows, you know. Shouldn't you like to know about them, Luke?'

'Nay, Miss, I'n got to keep 'count o' the flour an' corn – I can't do wi' knowin' so many things besides my work.

That's what brings folk to the gallows – knowin' everything but what they'd got to get their bread by. An' they're mostly lies, I think, what's printed i' the books: them printed sheets are, anyhow, as the men cry i' the streets.'

'Why you're like my brother, Tom, Luke,' said Maggie, wishing to turn the conversation agreeably. 'Tom's not fond of reading. I love Tom so dearly, Luke – better than anybody else in the world. When he grows up, I shall keep his house, and we shall always live together. I can tell him everything he doesn't know. But I think Tom's clever, for all he doesn't like books: he makes beautiful whip cord and rabbit pens.'

'Ah,' said Luke, 'but he'll be fine an' vexed as the rabbits are all dead.'

'Dead!' screamed Maggie, jumping up from her sliding seat on the corn. 'Oh, dear Luke! What, the lop-eared one, and the spotted doe, that Tom spent all his money to buy?'

'As dead as moles,' said Luke, fetching his comparison from the unmistakable corpses nailed to the stable wall.

'Oh dear Luke,' said Maggie, in a piteous tone, while the big tears rolled down her cheek, 'Tom told me to take care of 'em, and I forgot. What *shall* I do?'

'Well, you see, Miss, they war in that far toolhouse, an' it was nobody's business to see to 'em. I reckon Master Tom told Harry to feed 'em, but there's no countin' on Harry – *he*'s a offal creatur as iver come about the primises, he is. He remembers nothin' but his own inside – an' I wish it 'ud gripe him.'

'Oh Luke, Tom told me to be sure and remember the rabbits every day – but how could I, when they did not come into my head, you know? Oh, he will be so angry with me, I know he will, and so sorry about his rabbits – and so am I sorry. Oh what *shall* I do?'

'Don't you fret, Miss,' said Luke, soothingly, 'they're nash things, them lop-eared rabbits – they'd happen ha' died, if they'd been fed. Things out o' natur niver thrive. God A'lmighty doesn't like 'em. He made the rabbits' ears to lie back, an' it's nothin' but contrairiness to make 'em hing down like a mastiff dog's. Master Tom 'ull know better nor buy such things another time. Don't you fret, Miss. Will you come along home wi' me, and see my wife? I'm a-goin' this minute.'

The invitation offered an agreeable distraction to Maggie's grief, and her tears gradually subsided as she trotted along by Luke's side to his pleasant cottage, which stood with its apple and pear trees, and with the added dignity of a lean-to pigsty, close by the brink of the Ripple. Mrs Moggs, Luke's wife, was a decidedly agreeable acquaintance: she exhibited her hospitality in bread and treacle and possessed various works of art. Maggie actually forgot that she had any special cause of sadness this morning, as she stood on a chair to look at a remarkable series of pictures representing the Prodigal Son in the costume of Sir Charles Grandison, except that, as might have been expected from his defective moral character, he had not, like that accomplished hero, the taste and strength of mind to dispense with a wig. But the indefinable weight the dead rabbits had left on her mind caused her to feel more than usual pity for the career of this weak young man, particularly when she looked at the picture where he leaned against a tree with a flaccid appearance, his knee-breeches unbuttoned and his wig awry, while the swine, apparently of some foreign breed, seemed to insult him by their good spirits over their feast of husks.

ROBERT LOUIS STEVENSON

'Whole Duty of Children'

A child should always say what's true,
And speak when he is spoken to,
And behave mannerly at table:
At least as far as he is able.

REVEREND FRANCIS KILVERT

Diary

16th January 1875

In the Common Field in front of the cottages I found two little figures in the dusk. One tiny urchin was carefully binding a handkerchief round the face of an urchin even more tiny than himself. It was Fred and Jerry Savine. 'What are you doing to him?' I asked Fred. 'Please, Sir,' said the child solemnly; 'Please, Sir, we'm gwine to play at blindman's buff.' The two children were quite alone. The strip of dusky meadow was like a marsh and every footstep trod the water out of the soaked land, but the two little images went solemnly on with their game as if they were in a magnificent playground with a hundred children to play with.

Oh, the wealth of a child's imagination and capacity for enjoyment of trifles!

JOHN B. WATSON

from *Psychological Care of Infant and Child* (1928)

The ideal child is: A child who never cries unless actually stuck by a pin, illustratively speaking . . . who soon builds up a wealth of habits that tides him over dark and rainy days – who puts on such habits of politeness and neatness and cleanliness that adults are willing to be around him at least part of the day . . . who eats what is set before him – who sleeps and rests when put to bed for sleep and rest – who puts away two-year-old habits when the third year has to be faced . . . who finally enters manhood so bulwarked with stable work and emotional habits that no adversity can quite overwhelm him.

ISAAC BASHEVIS SINGER

The Reading Child

There are five hundred reasons why I began to write for children, but to save time I will mention only ten of them: Number 1. Children read books, not reviews. They don't give a hoot about the critics. Number 2. Children don't read to find their identity. Number 3. They don't read to free themselves of guilt, to quench their thirst for rebellion, or to get rid of alienation. Number 4. They have no use for psychology. Number 5. They detest sociology. Number 6. They don't try to understand Kafka or *Finnegans Wake*. Number 7. They still believe in God, the family, angels, devils, witches, goblins, logic, clarity, punctuation, and other such obsolete stuff. Number 8. They love interesting stories, not commentary, guides or footnotes. Number 9. When a book is boring they yawn openly, without any shame or fear of authority. Number 10. They don't expect their beloved writer to redeem humanity. Young as they are, they know that is not in his power. Only the adults have such childish illusions.

THOMAS HARDY

from *Jude the Obscure*

Sue sat looking at the bare floor of the room, the house being little more than an old intramural cottage, and then she regarded the scene outside the uncurtained window. At some distance opposite, the outer walls of Sarcophagus College – silent, black and windowless – threw their four centuries of gloom, bigotry and decay into the little room she occupied, shutting out the moonlight by night and the sun by day. The outlines of Rubric College also were discernible beyond the other, and the tower of a third further off still. She thought of the strange operation of a simple-minded man's ruling passion, that it should have led Jude, who loved her and the children so tenderly, to place them here in this depressing purlieu, because he was still haunted by this dream. Even now he did not distinctly hear the freezing negative that those scholared walls had echoed to his desire.

The failure to find another lodging, and the lack of room in this house for his father, had made a deep impression on the boy; a brooding undemonstrative horror seemed to have seized him. The silence was broken by his saying: 'Mother, *what* shall we do tomorrow!'

'I don't know!' said Sue despondently. 'I am afraid this will trouble your father.'

'I wish father was quite well, and there had been room for him! Then it wouldn't matter so much! Poor father!'

'It wouldn't!'

'Can I do anything?'

'No! All is trouble, adversity and suffering!'

'Father went away to give us children room, didn't he?'

'Partly.'

'It would be better to be out o' the world than in it, wouldn't it?'

'It would almost, dear.'

' 'Tis because of us children, too, isn't it, that you can't get a good lodging?'

'Well – people do object to children sometimes.'

'Then if children make so much trouble, why do people have 'em?'

'Oh – because it is a law of nature.'

'But we don't ask to be born?'

'No indeed.'

'And what makes it worse with me is that you are not my real mother, and you needn't have had me unless you liked. I oughtn't to have come to 'ee – that's the real truth! I troubled 'em in Australia, and I trouble folk here. I wish I hadn't been born!'

'You couldn't help it, my dear.'

'I think that whenever children be born that are not wanted they should be killed directly, before their souls come to 'em, and not allowed to grow big and walk about!'

Sue did not reply. She was doubtfully pondering how to treat this too reflective child.

She at last concluded that, so far as circumstances permitted, she would be honest and candid with one who entered into her difficulties like an aged friend.

'There is going to be another in our family soon,' she hesitatingly remarked.

'How?'

'There is going to be another baby.'

'What!' The boy jumped up wildly. 'Oh God, mother,

you've never a-sent for another; and such trouble with what you've got!'

'Yes, I have, I am sorry to say!' murmured Sue, her eyes glistening with suspended tears.

The boy burst out weeping. 'Oh, you don't care, you don't care!' he cried in bitter reproach. 'How *ever* could you, mother, be so wicked and cruel as this, when you needn't have done it till we was better off, and father well! To bring us all into *more* trouble! No room for us, and father a-forced to go away, and we turned out tomorrow; and yet you be going to have another of us soon! . . . 'Tis done o' purpose! – 'tis – 'tis!' He walked up and down sobbing.

'Y-you must forgive me, little Jude!' she pleaded, her bosom heaving now as much as the boy's. 'I can't explain – I will when you are older. It does seem – as if I had done it on purpose, now we are in these difficulties! I can't explain, dear! But it – is not quite on purpose – I can't help it!'

'Yes it is – it must be! For nobody would interfere with us, like that, unless you agreed! I won't forgive you, ever, ever! I'll never believe you care for me, or father, or any of us any more!'

He got up, and went away into the closet adjoining her room, in which a bed had been spread on the floor. There she heard him say: 'If we children was gone there'd be no trouble at all!'

'Don't think that, dear,' she cried, rather peremptorily. 'But go to sleep!'

The following morning she awoke at a little past six, and decided to get up and run across before breakfast to the inn which Jude had informed her to be his quarters, to tell him what had happened before he went out. She arose softly, to avoid disturbing the children, who, as she knew, must be fatigued by their exertions of yesterday.

She found Jude at breakfast in the obscure tavern he had chosen as a counterpoise to the expense of her lodging: and she explained to him her homelessness. He had been so anxious about her all night, he said. Somehow, now it was morning, the request to leave the lodgings did not seem such a depressing incident as it had seemed the night before, nor did even her failure to find another place affect her so deeply as at first. Jude agreed with her that it would not be worth while to insist upon her right to stay a week, but to take immediate steps for removal.

'You must all come to this inn for a day or two,' he said. 'It is a rough place, and it will not be so nice for the children, but we shall have more time to look round. There are plenty of lodgings in the suburbs – in my old quarter of Beersheba. Have breakfast with me now you are here, my bird. You are sure you are well? There will be plenty of time to get back and prepare the chldren's meal before they wake. In fact, I'll go with you.'

She joined Jude in a hasty meal, and in a quarter of an hour they started together, resolving to clear out from Sue's too respectable lodging immediately. On reaching the place and going upstairs she found that all was quiet in the children's room, and called to the landlady in timorous tones to please bring up the tea kettle and something for their breakfast. This was perfunctorily done, and producing a couple of eggs which she had brought with her she put them into the boiling kettle, and summoned Jude to watch them for the youngsters, while she went to call them, it being now about half past eight o'clock.

Jude stood bending over the kettle, with his watch in his hand, timing the eggs, so that his back was turned to the little inner chamber where the children lay. A shriek from Sue suddenly caused him to start round. He saw that the door of the room, or rather closet – which had seemed to go heavily upon its hinges as she pushed it back – was open, and that Sue had sunk to the floor just within it. Hastening forward to pick her up he turned his eyes to the little bed spread on the boards; no children were there. He looked in bewilderment round the room.

At the back of the door were fixed two hooks for hanging garments, and from these the forms of the two youngest children were suspended, by a piece of box cord round each of their necks, while from a nail a few yards off the body of little Jude was hanging in a similar manner. An overturned chair was near the elder boy, and his glazed eyes were slanted into the room; but those of the girl and the baby were closed.

Half paralysed by the strange and consummate horror of the scene he let Sue lie, cut the cords with his pocket-knife and threw the three children on the bed; but the feel of their bodies in the momentary handling seemed to say that they were dead. He caught up Sue, who was in fainting fits, and put her on the bed in the other room, after which he breathlessly summoned the landlady and ran out for a doctor.

When he got back Sue had come to herself, and the two helpless women, bending over the chldren in wild efforts to restore them, and the triplet of little corpses, formed a sight which overthrew his self-command. The nearest surgeon came in, but, as Jude had inferred, his presence was superfluous. The children were past saving, for though their bodies were still barely cold it was conjectured that they had been hanging more than an hour. The probability held by the parents later on, when they were able to reason on the case, was that the elder boy, on waking, looked into the outer room for Sue, and, finding her absent, was thrown into a fit of aggravated despondency that the events and information of the evening before had induced in his morbid temperament. Moreover a piece of paper was found upon the floor, on which was written, in the boy's hand, with a bit of lead pencil that he carried:

Done because we are too menny.

At sight of this Sue's nerves utterly gave way, an awful conviction that her discourse with the boy had been the main cause of the tragedy throwing her into a convulsive agony which knew no abatement. They carried her away against her wish to a room on the lower floor: and there she lay, her slight figure shaken with her gasps, and her eyes staring at the ceiling, the woman of the house vainly trying to soothe her.

They could hear from this chamber the people moving about above, and she implored to be allowed to go back, and was only kept from doing so by the assurance that, if there were any hope, her presence might do harm, and the reminder that it was necessary to take care of herself lest she should endanger a coming life. Her inquiries were incessant, and at last Jude came down and told her there was no hope. As soon as she could speak she informed him what she had said to the boy, and how she thought herself to cause of this.

'No,' said Jude. 'It was in his nature to do it. The doctor says there are such boys springing up amongst us – boys of a sort unknown in the last generation – the outcome of new views of life. They seem to see all its terrors before they are old enough to have staying power to resist them. He says it is the beginning of the coming universal wish not to live. He's an advanced man, the doctor: but he can give no consolation to—'

Jude had kept back his own grief on account of her; but he now broke down; and this stimulated Sue to efforts of sympathy which in some degree distracted her from her poignant self-reproach. When everybody was gone, she was allowed to see the children.

The boy's face expressed the whole tale of their situation. On that little shape had converged all the inauspiciousness and shadow which had darkened the first union of Jude, and all the accidents, mistakes, fears, errors of the last. He was their nodal point, their focus, their expression in a single term. For the rashness of those parents he had groaned, for their ill-assortment he had quaked, and for the misfortunes of these he had died.

When the house was silent, and they could do nothing

but await the coroner's inquest, a subdued, large, low voice spread into the air of the room from behind the heavy walls at the back.

'What is it?' said Sue, her spasmodic breathing suspended.

'The organ of the College chapel. The organist practising I suppose. It's the anthem from the seventy-third Psalm: "Truly God is loving unto Israel".'

She sobbed again, 'Oh, oh my babies! They had done no harm! Why should they have been taken away, and not I!'

There was another stillness – broken at last by two persons in conversation somewhere without.

'They are talking about us, no doubt!' moaned Sue. '"We are made a spectacle unto the world, and to angels, and to men!"'

Jude listened – 'No – they are not talking of us,' he said. 'They are two clergymen of different views, arguing about the eastward position. Good God – the eastward position, and all creation groaning!'

Then another silence, till she was seized with another uncontrollable fit of grief. 'There is something external to us which says, "You shan't!" First it said, "You shan't learn!" Then it said, "You shan't labour!" Now it says, "You shan't love!"'

He tried to soothe her by saying, 'That's bitter of you, darling.'

'But it's true!'

Thus they waited, and she went back again to her room. The baby's frock, shoes and socks, which had been lying on a chair at the time of his death, she would not now have removed, though Jude would fain have got them out of her sight. But whenever he touched them she implored him to let them lie, and burst out almost savagely at the woman of the house when she also attempted to put them away.

Jude dreaded her dull apathetic silences almost more than her paroxysms. 'Why don't you speak to me,

Jude?' she cried out, after one of these. 'Don't turn away from me! I can't *bear* the loneliness of being out of your looks!'

'There, dear; here I am,' he said, putting his face close to hers.

'Yes . . . Oh my comrade, our perfect union – our two-in-oneness – is now stained with blood!'

'Shadowed by death – that's all.'

'Ah; but it was I who incited him really, though I didn't know I was doing it! I talked to the chlid as one should only talk to people of mature age. I said the world was against us, that it was better to be out of life than in it at this price; and he took it literally. And I told him I was going to have another child. It upset him. Oh how bitterly he upbraided me!'

'Why did you do it, Sue?'

'I can't tell. It was that I wanted to be truthful. I couldn't bear deceiving him as to the facts of life. And yet I wasn't truthful, for with a false delicacy I told him too obscurely. Why was I half wiser than my fellow women? And not entirely wiser! Why didn't I tell him pleasant untruths, instead of half realities? It was my want of self-control, so that I could neither conceal things nor reveal them!'

'Your plan might have been a good one for the majority of cases; only in our peculiar case it chanced to work badly perhaps. He must have known sooner or later.'

'And I was just making my baby darling a new frock; and now I shall never see him in it, and never talk to him any more! . . . My eyes are so swollen that I can scarcely see; and yet little more than a year ago I called myself happy! We went about loving each other too much – indulging ourselves to utter selfishness with each other! We said – do you remember? – that we would make a virtue of joy. I said it was Nature's intention, Nature's law and *raison d'être* that we should be joyful in what instincts she afforded us – instincts which civilization had taken upon itself to thwart.

What dreadful things I said! And now Fate has given us this stab in the back for being such fools as to take Nature at her word!'

She sank into a quiet contemplation, till she said, 'It is best, perhaps, that they should be gone. Yes – I see it is! Better that they should be plucked fresh than to stay to wither away miserably!'

'Yes,' replied Jude. 'Some say that the elders should rejoice when their children die in infancy.'

'But they don't know! ... Oh my babies, my babies, could you be alive now! You may say the boy wished to be out of life, or he wouldn't have done it. It was not unreasonable for him to die: it was part of his incurably sad nature, poor little fellow! But then the others – my *own* children and yours!'

Again Sue looked at the hanging little frock, and at the socks and shoes; and her figure quivered like a string. 'I am a pitiable creature,' she said, 'good neither for earth nor heaven any more! I am driven out of my mind by things! What ought to be done?' She stared at Jude, and tightly held his hand.

'Nothing can be done,' he replied. 'Things are as they are, and will be brought to their destined issue.'

She paused. 'Yes! Who said that?' she asked heavily.

'It comes in the chorus of the *Agamemnon*. It has been in my mind continually since this happened.'

'My poor Jude – how you've missed everything! – you more than I, for I did get you! To think you should know that by your unassisted reading, and yet be in poverty and despair!'

After such momentary diversions her grief would return in a wave.

The jury duly came and viewed the bodies, the inquest was held; and next arrived the melancholy morning of the funeral. Accounts in the newspapers had brought to the spot curious idlers, who stood apparently counting the windowpanes and the stones of the walls. Doubt of the real relations of the couple added zest to their curiosity. Sue had declared that she would follow the two little ones to the grave, but at the last moment she gave way, and the coffins were quietly carried out of the house while she was lying down. Jude got into the vehicle, and it drove away, much to the relief of the landlord, who now had only Sue and her luggage remaining on his hands, which he hoped to be also clear of later on in the day, and so to have freed his house from the exasperating notoriety it had acquired during the week through his wife's unlucky admission of these strangers. In the afternoon he privately consulted with the owner of the house, and they agreed that if any objection to it arose from the tragedy which had occurred there they would try to get its number changed.

When Jude had seen the two little boxes – one containing little Jude, and the other the two smallest – deposited in the earth he hastened back to Sue, who was still in her room, and he therefore did not disturb her just then. Feeling anxious, however, he went again about four o'clock. The woman thought she was still lying down, but returned to him to say that she was not in her bedroom after all. Her hat and jacket, too, were missing: she had gone out. Jude hurried off to the public house where he was sleeping. She had not been there. Then bethinking himself of possibilities he went along the road to the cemetery, which he entered, and crossed to where the interments had recently taken place. The idlers who had followed to the spot by reason of the tragedy were all gone now. A man with a shovel in his hands was attempting to earth in the common grave of the three children, but his arm was held back by an expostulating woman who stood in the half-filled hole. It was Sue, whose coloured clothing, which she had never thought of changing for the mourning he had bought, suggested to the eye a deeper grief than the conventional garb of bereavement could express.

'He's filling them in, and he shan't till I've seen my little ones again!' she cried wildly when she saw Jude. 'I want to see them once more. Oh Jude – please Jude – I want to see them! I didn't know you would let them be taken away while I was asleep! You said perhaps I should see them once more before they were screwed down; and then you didn't, but took them away! Oh Jude, you are cruel to me too!'

'She's been wanting me to dig out the grave again, and let her get to the coffins,' said the man with the spade. 'She ought to be took home, by the look o' her. She is hardly responsible, poor thing, seemingly. Can't dig 'em up again now, ma'am. Do ye go home with your husband, and take it quiet, and thank God that there'll be another soon to swage yer grief.'

But Sue kept asking piteously: 'Can't I see them once more – just once! Can't I? Only just one little minute, Jude? It would not take long! And I should be so glad, Jude! I will be so good, and not disobey you ever any more, Jude, if you will let me? I would go home quietly afterwards, and not want to see them any more! Can't I? Why can't I?'

Thus she went on. Jude was thrown into such acute sorrow that he almost felt he would try to get the man to accede. But it could do no good, and might make her still worse; and he saw that it was imperative to get her home at once. So he coaxed her, and whispered tenderly, and put his arm round her to support her; till she helplessly gave in, and was induced to leave the cemetery.

He wished to obtain a fly to take her back in, but economy being so imperative she deprecated his doing so, and they walked along slowly. Jude in black crape, she in brown and red clothing. They were to have gone to a new lodging that afternoon, but Jude saw that it was not practicable, and in course of time they entered the now hated house. Sue was at once got to bed, and the doctor sent for.

Jude waited all the evening downstairs. At a very late

hour the intelligence was brought to him that a child had been prematurely born, and that it, like the others, was a corpse.

GEORGE ELIOT

from *The Mill on the Floss*

Childhood has no forebodings; but then it is soothed by no memories of outlived sorrow.

MICHAEL ROSEN

'Song'

My boyfriend gave me an apple,
my boyfriend gave me a pear,
my boyfriend gave me a kiss on the lips
and threw me down the stairs.

I gave him back his apple,
I gave him back his pear,
I gave him back his kiss on the lips
and I threw him down the stairs.

He took me to the pictures,
To see a sexy film,
and when I wasn't looking
he kissed another girl.

I threw him over Italy,
I threw him over France.
I threw him over Germany
and he landed on his arse.

WALTER DE LA MARE

'The Sleeping Child'

Like night-shut flower is this slumbering face,
  Lamplight, for moon, upon its darkness spying;
That wheat-stook hair, the gold-fringed lids, the grace
  Of body entranced, and without motion lying.

Passive as fruit the rounded cheek; bright lip;
  The zigzag turquoise of that artery straying;
Thridding the chartless labyrinths of sleep,
  River of life in fount perpetual playing.

Magical light! though we are leagues apart,
  My stealthiest whisper would at once awake thee!
Not I, thou angel thing! At peace thou art.
  And childhood's dreams, at least, need not forsake thee.

YOUTH

OSCAR WILDE

Children begin by loving their parents; after a time they judge them; rarely, if ever, do they forgive them.

MARY KARR

from *The Liars Club*

For two days before the storm came inland, folks had been getting ready. Weather reports got scarier. Windows were boarded up with sheet of plywood. Bags were packed. The supermarket had runs on batteries and candles and canned beans. Higher ground was just about anywhere else, and people were heading for it. Transistor radios repeated over and over that this was a Class Four hurricane. Nobody wanted to ride that out. A lot of families took time to root around in their attics to rescue special photographs and papers like marriage licenses from the tidal wave that Cattleman Bill was calling inevitable. I remember Carol Sharp's mother wrapped her baby shoes up in tissue paper to take along.

We did none of these things. Daddy tended to shrug about a storm. 'Shit, if it hits here, it'll take the house,' he said. He didn't figure there was much point in scrabbling around, since a direct hit would wipe us out anyway. Which attitude didn't go far toward reassuring me. While other fathers were taking sick leave and folding up their lawn chairs and storing special furniture high in their attics, Daddy just kept plodding off to the plant and coming home long enough to refill his mess kit with food and plodding back. Eventually, he didn't bother coming home at all.

It's odd to me now how easily I let him leave our lives that fall at such an ugly time. Maybe he'd been slowly backpedaling out of the daddy business since Grandma came. Things just ran smoother without him around for the old woman to carp at. Maybe his absence was inevitable as we got older.

In fairness to Daddy, we at that point had plenty of time to evacuate, so it's not like the storm threatened our lives or anything, just our property, which didn't actually amount to much dollarwise. Plus the Gulf Oil Corporation kept those men who hadn't run off with their families working more or less nonstop, at double overtime, trying to get the plant battened down. Daddy would have felt like a fool turning that down. Still, I wonder why we loosened our grip on him so easy. Having Mother take care of us without him meant that – with the right amount of whining – we could talk her into buying nearly any toy, article of clothing, or treat. She saw us as grossly underprivileged. We were practically urchins, by her standards. So, in her care, we did things that Daddy, with his forty-acres-and-a-mule sense of thrift, wouldn't have stood for: cutting up a sheet over a card table for a playhouse, say, or painting murals on the garage wall with oil paints. Daddy had an extravagance of heart. He pretty much indulged us in a way neighbors found shameful. But he drew a hard line at anything that seemed to waste money, which was where Mother started to overtake him in our hearts.

The first day that he didn't come home at all, Lecia and I called him a bunch of times. I always imagined our voices snailing through the telephone lines in an intricate pattern of stops and transfers trying to get to him. 'Gulf Oil. Hep you?' was how the operator answered at the first ring. 'Extension 691, please,' we'd tell her. Lecia and I would stand nearly ear to ear in the kitchen, each one trying to squeeze the other off the receiver. Our forearms, on this day, got covered with little half-moon bruises where we'd pinched each other trying to hog the whole receiver. He would always talk as long as we wanted, but he wouldn't come home, no matter how we whined or begged. I remember his saying, 'You take care of your momma,' and my asking who was going to take care of us. (Which I don't remember his answering.) Right before he hung up, Lecia suggested that he talk to Mother himself – maybe hoping he'd get the idea that she didn't quite have both oars in the water. At that point, he claimed somebody was calling him and just hung up.

By that afternoon, the town was emptying itself of people, and still we didn't leave. The news reports were getting real specific. They showed the tidal surges that wiped out the beach road. They showed the cars bumper to bumper heading upcountry over the Orange Bridge. People evacuated with their headlights on in daylight like it was all some town-side funeral procession.

The next morning, the front page of the paper carried a shot of palm trees snapped off at Crystal Beach. School got closed, so Lecia and I sat around the house making puppets from paper bags and watching endless TV: *I Love Lucy*, *Leave It to Beaver*, all family sitcoms where the dads walked around in suit jackets and the women wore heels to vacuum all day.

Cattleman Bill himself had disappeared from that morning's news. In his place stood the stout and sweating sportscaster wearing his button-bulging suit and skinny tie. He told us that the front end of the storm would hit us by noon. 'You are advised to seek shelter,' he said. 'Repeat. You are advised to seek shelter.' He had that terrific sort of self-importance in making the announcement, like Barney Fife on *Andy Griffith* pretending he was some tough-guy detective instead of a small-town deputy in charge of the school crossing. About half an hour after this newscast, they set the tornado sirens blowing.

Some of the local church folks had been preaching the world's end in that storm. Carol Sharp gave me all the details in her front yard before her family evacuated. We were standing under the mimosa tree at the time. Its pink hairy blossoms were falling all around us in the wind, and her daddy and mother were roping down a tarp over the roof of their Chevy. Carol described how the Four Horseman of the Apocalypse would come riding down out of the clouds with their black capes flapping behind them, and how the burning pit would open up in the earth for sinners like me, and how Jesus would lead her and her family right up a golden stair to heaven. Some evangelist had put his hand on her forehead the day before, and that very instant a seed wart on her right thumb had up and vanished. I had personally done surgery on that wart, picking the seeds out of it with a straight pin not a week before, and sure enough, there was no trace of it that morning. Which gave me pause. But I was spiteful enough to tell her that I didn't much want to sign up with any god who sent tidal waves crashing down on trailer parks but took time for her old wart. (Despite my breathtaking gullibility, I was able to spew out such random hunks of elementary logic sometimes.)

Back home, the light in our windows was gradually turning a darker and darker shade of charcoal. Mother was hanging draperies over the big picture window, and through that window, I could see the Sharps' Chevy backing out of their driveway, tarp and all. *What if old Mr Sharp's right about God and Jesus?* I must have said out loud. Or maybe I suggested we pray just in case – I don't remember. What's dead clear now is how Mother lifted her middle finger to the ceiling and said, Oh, fuck that God! Between that and the tornado sirens and the black sky that had slid over all our windows and Grandma stone deaf to that blasphemy because she was tatting those weensy stitches, I began to think we'd be washed out to sea for all our sins at any minute.

Lecia must have gotten scared too, because she started lobbying for us to get in the car and drive to Aunt Iris's house right away. Daddy's sister lived sixty miles north in the hills outside Kirbyville. 'Let's just go,' she kept saying. I remember she argued that the big traffic had already died down. She even tried to talk to Grandma, who was lost in her lacemaking.

Daddy called about then, and Mother surprised us by picking up the phone herself. I remember that she had a dish towel in one hand, and she sounded pissed off that he was calling at all. She told him that the car was running outside, that we were walking out the door that very minute. In fact, she hadn't even hauled her daddy's Gladstone bag out of the closet yet. The TV was blaring *Dennis the Menace*. I was sitting on the floor with Lecia, cutting fringe on a paper-bag Indian costume, when Mother slammed down the receiver.

Now I know she needed him there that day, and her fury was the closest she could get to an invitation. Daddy was lost to us in that fury. The line was severed, and in the mist that occupied my skull that morning, he floated away, getting smaller and smaller. I looked over to Lecia, who shrugged and went back to cutting her fringe with a sick precision. At that instant, I knew we should have evacuated long before. The slow psychic weight of doom settled over me.

Mother later explained to us that we would have gone at sunrise, but Grandma for some reason refused to leave. She got it in her head that there was only a little rain shower coming. It was as if her lifelong terror of storms had imploded somehow and left her believing that a Class Four hurricane moving directly across our house couldn't budge her. Even the nice young Guardsman in the camouflage suit who came to stand in our living room with his bullhorn at his side didn't rile her up. 'We appreciate your stopping by,' she said, trying to herd him out of the house by bumping the backs of his knees with her chair wheels. By this time, Mother sat at the dining table sobbing and wiping at her face with that dish towel. The soldier finally threatened to pick Grandma up physically and tote her to the car, to which she said okay, she'd go, but she had to take a bath first. He said that he reckoned they'd already stopped water service, but Lecia got the water running, and Grandma wheeled herself in there and shut the door.

It was when that door clicked shut that Lecia decided to call Daddy to come get us out of there. Right that minute. But the phone line had gone dead. I saw the shock of this fact on her face before she even handed me the receiver. (Lecia was nothing if not cool in a crisis. She learned to drive at twelve, at which age I once saw her convince a state trooper that she'd just left her license at home because she was running out to get her baby milk while he was still sleeping.) But her expression that morning with the black phone at her ear betrayed her age. Her eyes got shiny for a second. She was really only nine, after all, and what with the tornado sirens wailing the way our music teacher had warned they would only when the Russian missiles were launched from Cuba, and the phone line to Daddy snapped dead, Lecia looked ready to give up the grown-up act altogether.

She handed me the phone. She didn't want to be alone in knowing how alone we were, so she handed it to me, so I'd know too. And that flat silence right up against my ear brought it all home to me. You never notice how hooked up to everybody you feel when you hear that rush of air under the dial tone, as if all the world's circuits are just waiting to hear you – anyway, you never notice that till it goes away. Then it's like you listen, expecting that faraway sound, and instead you get only the numb quiet of your own skull not knowing what to think of next.

It was the National Guardsman who wound up getting us out. He came back about when the rain had started to blow sideways against all the windows with a sound like BB pellets. Grandma's bath had wound up taking too long. Mother let him force the bathroom door with a screwdriver, and there Grandma sat unmoved from her chair, all her attention honed to that shuttle of hers manufacturing lace while bathwater poured over the edges of the tub and on to the floor.

He did have to pick her up, finally. He swooped her up in his arms like she was a bride. Her good leg hung down normally enough, but her stump kept slipping down past his elbow and starting to dangle. Lecia and I had a giggle fit over this on the porch, because Grandma's legs kept splaying open in a way she would have found unladylike.

Outside, the wind had set the phone lines to swaying. It had already started to tear loose some shingles that were blowing up the street. Plus gusts somehow squirmed into the window cracks to make a high-pitched whistling that seemed to get louder by the second. Lecia and I ran for the car, a distance of ten yards, and got drenched to the skin. Getting in the car was like leaving the first big noise of the storm and sitting in a cold bubble. We could barely see the Guardsman through the water streaming off the windshield. He seemed somehow to be trying to move in a more gallant or stately way, what with Grandma's leg slipping down every other step and all. Anyway, he was slower than we had been, which made us laugh. But we stopped giggling pretty quick when Mother slid behind the wheel.

You could see by her eyes in the rearview that she wasn't crying any more. That had come to be a bad sign, the not crying. Her mouth turned into a neat little hyphen.

I watched the Guardsman climb back in his jeep; then the grey and the rain sort of gobbled up everything but a big olive-drab smear that was moving out of our driveway behind us. I had this crazy urge to roll down my window and poke my head right out into the storm and holler to him to come back. But the wind would have eaten any words I yelled. So I watched the smear of his jeep get littler. Then it was gone, and there was just rain and sirens and Mother's cold grey eyes set smack in the middle of that silver oblong mirror.

The drive from Leechfield to Aunt Iris's house in Kirbyville would normally have taken an hour. That's in the best weather conditions. 'Sixty minutes, door to door' was what Daddy always said climbing out of his truck cab or stepping up on their porch. (I once made the trip dead drunk on a summer morning in a souped-up Mustang in forty-five minutes, and I never got under eighty, slowed for a curve, or stopped for a light.) This particular day it took fifty-five minutes. Lecia timed it. That's in blinding rain, rain so heavy the wipers never really showed you the road. They just slapped over the blur and then slapped back to reveal more blur. Sure, we must have had wind at our backs. Still, I figure that Mother drove through the first onslaught of a hurricane with the gas pedal pressed flush to the floorboard, without a nickel's worth of hesitation. Maybe she knew that her mother was close to dying and just didn't care if we made it to high ground in one piece or not. We were late enough leaving town that there were no other vehicles on the road, which was good. Doubtless we would have hit them had they been there. Only shit-house luck kept us from sliding sideways off the narrow blacktop and into one of the umpteen jillion bayous we passed. For a good five miles out of town, you could hear the sirens getting littler, so the roar of the wind got bigger. That made it seem like we were heading into the storm instead of away from it.

When we hit Port Arthur, Texas, Mother started to sing under her breath. It was an old song she liked to play on our turntable when she was drinking. She had a scratchy recording of Peggy Lee or Della Reese, one of those whiskey-voice lounge singers:

> Oh the shark has zippy teeth, dear,
> And he shows them pearly white.
> Just a jack knife has his teeth, dear,
> And he keeps them out of sight . . .

Nobody in my family can sing a note. The few times we went to church with neighbours, Lecia and I had the good sense to lip-synch the hymns so it wouldn't be too noticeable. My mother, too, had a bad voice – wavery and vague.

She was a natural alto who'd probably been nagged into the higher ranges by overfeminine choir teachers. So she sang the wrong words in a ragged soprano under her breath that morning, whispery and high. The car seemed to pick up speed as she sang, and the fear that had been nuzzling around my solar plexus all morning started to get real definite when I saw, dead ahead of us, the gray steel girders of the Orange Bridge.

The Orange Bridge at that time was said to be the highest bridge in the country. Your ears popped when you drove over it. The engineers had built it that tall so that even tugs shoving oil platforms with full sized derricks on them could pass under with room to spare. The Sabine River it ran over wasn't very wide, so the bridge had easily the sharpest incline of any I've ever crossed.

Not surprisingly, this was the scene of a suicide every year or so. Jilted suitors and bankrupt oilmen favored it. Those who jumped from the highest point of the bridge broke every bone in their bodies. I remember Mother reading this fact out loud from the paper one time, then saying that women tended to gas themselves or take sleeping pills – things that didn't mess them up on the outside so much. She liked to quote James Dean about leaving a beautiful corpse.

Anyway, it was this bridge that the car bumped onto with Mother singing the very scariest part of 'Mack the Knife'. She sang it very whispery, like a lullaby:

> When the shark bites with his teeth, dear,
> Scarlet billows start to spread . . .

The car tipped way back when we mounted the bridge. It felt sort of like the long climb a roller coaster will start before its deep fall. Mother's singing immediately got drowned out by the steel webbing under the tires that made the whole car shimmy. At the same time – impossibly enough – we seemed to be going faster.

Lecia contends that at this point I started screaming, and that my screaming prompted Mother to wheel around and start grabbing at me, which caused what happened next. (Were Lecia writing this memoir, I would appear in one of only three guises: sobbing hyterically, wetting my pants in a deliberately inconvenient way, or biting somebody, usually her, with no provocation.)

I don't recall that Mother reached around to grab at me at all. And I flatly deny screaming. But despite my old trick of making my stomach into a rock, I did get carsick. The bile started rising in my throat the second we mounted the bridge, which involved the car flying over a metal rise that felt like a ski jump. We landed with a jolt and then fishtailed a little.

I knew right away that I was going to throw up. Still, I tried locking down my belly the way I had on the Tilt-A-Whirl. I squinched my eyes shut. I bore down on myself inside. But the rolling in my stomach wouldn't let me get ahold of it. I wouldn't have opened my window on a dare. And I sure didn't want to ask mother to pull over mid-bridge. Lecia was in charge of all Mother-negotiations that day anyway, and she had opted for the same tooth-grinding silence we'd all fallen into. Even though she was normally devout about watching the speedometer and nagging Mother to slow down (or, conversely, Daddy to speed up), she kept her lip zipped that morning. Anyway, at the point when I felt the Cheerios start to rise in my throat, I just ducked my head, pulled the neck of my damp T-shirt over my nose and away from my body a little, and barfed down my shirt front. It was very warm sliding down my chest under the wet shirt, and it smelled like sour milk.

Mother responded to this not at all. Neither did Grandma, who had a nose like a bloodhound but had turned into some kind of manniquin. Really, she might have been carved from Ivory soap for all the color she had. Lecia would normally have seized the opportunity to whack me for being so gross. Maybe I even wanted whacking, at that point. Surely I wanted to break the bubble of quiet. But Lecia just tied her red bandana around her nose like a bank robber and shot me a sideways look. I knew then it was one of Mother's worst days, when my horking down my own shirt didn't warrant a word from anybody. Lecia watched Mother, who watched some bleary semblance of road.

Anyway, that's the last thing I remember before the crash – Lecia's bandana drawn over her nose.

JAMES BOSWELL

from *Diary*, c. 1770

At night, after we were in bed, Veronica spoke out from her little bed and said, 'I do not believe there is a God.' 'Preserve me,' said I, 'my dear, what do you mean?' She answered, 'I have *thinket* it many a time, but did not like to speak of it.' I was confounded and uneasy, and tried her with the simple Argument that without God there would not be all the things we see. It is He who makes the sun shine. Said She, 'It shines only on good days.' Said I: 'God made you'. Said she: 'My Mother bore me.' It was a strange and alarming thing to her Mother and me to hear our little Angel talk thus.

ELIZABETH BARRETT BROWNING

'The Cry of the Children'

Do ye hear the children weeping, O my brothers,
    Ere the sorrow comes with years?
They are leaning their young heads against their mothers,
    And *that* cannot stop their tears.
The young lambs are bleating in the meadows,
  The young birds are chirping in the nest,
The young fawns are playing with the shadows,
  The young flowers are blowing toward the west –
But the young, young children, O my brothers,
    They are weeping bitterly!
They are weeping in the playtime of the others,
    In the country of the free.

Do you question the young children in the sorrow
    Why their tears are falling so?
The old man may weep for his tomorrow
    Which is lost in Long Ago;
The old tree if leafless in the forest,
  The old year is ending in the frost,
The old wound, if stricken, is the sorest,
  The old hope is hardest to be lost:
But the young, young children, O my brothers,
    Do you ask them why they stand
Weeping sore before the bosoms of their mothers,
    In our happy Fatherland?

They look up with their pale and sunken faces,
And their looks are sad to see,
For the man's hoary anguish draws and presses
Down the cheeks of infancy;
'Your old earth,' they say, 'is very dreary,
Our young feet,' they say, 'are very weak;
Few paces have we taken, yet are weary –
Our grave-rest is very far to seek:
Ask the aged why they weep, and not the children,
For the outside earth is cold,
And we young ones stand without, in our bewildering,
And the graves are for the old.

'True,' say the children, 'it may happen
That we die before our time:
Little Alice died last year, her grave is shapen
Like a snowball, in the rime.
We looked into the pit prepared to take her:
Was no room for any work in the close clay!
From the sleep wherein she lieth none will wake her,
Crying, "Get up, little Alice! it is day."
If you listen by that grave, in sun and shower,
With your ear down, little Alice never cries;
Could we see her face, be sure we should not know her,
For the smile has time for growing in her eyes:
And merry go her moments, lulled and stilled in
The shroud by the kirk-chime.
'It is good when it happens,' say the children,
'That we die before our time.'

Alas, alas, the children! they are seeking
Death in life, as best to have:
They are binding up their hearts away from breaking,
With a cerement from the grave.
Go out, children, from the mine and from the city,
Sing out, children, as the little thrushes do;

Pluck your handfuls of the meadow-cowslips pretty,
Laugh aloud, to feel your fingers let them through!
But they answer: 'Are your cowslips of the meadows
Like our weeds anear the mine?
Leave us quiet in the dark of the coal-shadows,
From your pleasures fair and fine!

'For oh,' say the children, 'we are weary,
And we cannot run or leap;
If we cared for any meadows, it were merely
To drop down in them and sleep.
Our knees tremble sorely in the stooping,
We fall upon our faces, trying to go;
And, underneath our heavy eyelids drooping
The reddest flower would look as pale as snow.
For, all day, we drag our burden tiring
Through the coal-dark, underground;
Or, all day, we drive the wheels of iron
In the factories, round and round.

'For all day the wheels are droning, turning;
Their wind comes in our faces,
Till our hearts turn, our heads with pulses burning,
And the walls turn in their places:
Turns the sky in the high window, blank and reeling,
Turns the long light that drops adown the wall,
Turn the black flies that crawl along the ceiling:
All are turning, all the day, and we with all.
And all day the iron wheels are droning,
And sometimes we could pray,
"Oh ye wheels" (breaking out in a mad moaning),
"Stop! be silent for today!"'

Ay, be silent! Let them hear each other breathing
For a moment, mouth to mouth!
Let them touch each other's hands, in a fresh wreathing
Of their tender human youth!

Let them feel that this cold metallic motion
  Is not all the life God fashions or reveals:
Let them prove their living souls against the notion
  That they live in you, or under you, O wheels!
Still, all day, the iron wheels go onward,
    Grinding life down from its mark;
And the children's souls which God is calling sunward,
    Spin on blindly in the dark.

Now tell the poor young children, O my brothers,
    To look up to Him and pray;
So the blessed One who blesseth all the others,
    Will bless them another day.
They answer, 'Who is God that He should hear us,
  While the rushing of the iron wheels is stirred?
When we sob aloud, the human creatures near us
  Pass by, hearing not, or answer not a word.
And *we* hear not (for the wheels in their resounding)
    Strangers speaking at the door:
Is it likely God, with angels singing round Him,
    Hears our weeping any more?

'Two words, indeed, of praying we remember,
    And at midnight's hour of harm,
"Our Father", looking upward in the chamber,
    We say softly for a charm.
We know no other words except "Our Father",
  And we think that, in some pause of angels' song,
God may pluck them with the silence sweet to gather,
    And hold both within His right hand which is strong.
"Our Father!" If He heard us, He would surely
    (For they call Him good and mild)
Answer, smiling down the steep world very purely,
    "Come and rest with me, my child."

'But, no!' say the children, weeping faster,
    'He is speechless as a stone:

And they tell us, of His image is the master
        Who commands us to work on.
Go to!' say the children – 'up in Heaven,
    Dark, wheel-like, turning clouds are all we find.
Do not mock us; grief has made us unbelieving:
    We look up for God, but tears have made us blind.'
Do you hear the children weeping and disproving,
        O my brothers, what ye preach?
For God's possible is taught by His world's loving,
        And the children doubt of each.

And well may the children weep before you!
        They are weary ere they run;
They have never seen the sunshine, nor the glory
        Which is brighter than the sun.
They know the grief of man, without its wisdom;
    They sink in man's despair, without its calm;
Are slaves, without the liberty in Christdom,
    Are martyrs, by the pang without the palm:
Are worn as if with age, yet unretrievingly
        The harvest of its memories cannot reap –
Are orphans of the earthly love and heavenly.
        Let them weep! let them weep!

They look up with their pale and sunken faces,
        And their look is dread to see,
For they mind you of their angels in high places,
        With eyes turned on Deity.
'How long,' they say, 'how long, O cruel nation,
    Will you stand, to move the world, on a child't heart –
Stifle down with a mailed heel its palpitation,
    And tread onward to your throne amid the mart?
Our blood splashes upward, O gold-heaper,
        And your purple shows your path!
But the child's sob in the silence curses deeper
        Than the strong man in his wrath.'

SAMUEL RICHARDSON

I was not eleven years old when I wrote, spontaneously, a letter to a widow of near fifty, who, pretending to a zeal for religion, and who was a constant frequenter of church ordinances, was continually fomenting quarrels and disturbances by backbiting and scandal among all her acquaintance. I collected from the Scripture texts that made against her. Assuming the style and address of a person in years, I exhorted her; I expostulated with her. But my handwriting was known: I was challenged with it, and owned the boldness; for she complained of it to my mother with tears. My mother chid me for the freedom taken by such a boy with a woman of her years. But knowing that her son was not of a pert or forward nature, but, on the contrary, shy and bashful, she commended my principles, though she censured the liberty taken.

As a bashful and not forward boy, I was an early favourite with all the young women of taste and reading in the neighbourhood. Half a dozen of them then met to work with their needles, used, when they got a book they liked, and thought I should, to borrow me to read to them, their mothers sometimes with them; and both mothers and daughters used to be pleased with the observations they put me upon making.

I was not more than thirteen when three of these young women, unknown to each other, having an high opinion of my taciturnity, revealed to me their love secrets in order to induce me to give them copies to write after, or correct, for answer to their lovers' letters. Nor did any one of them ever know that I was the secretary to the others. I have been directed to chide, and even repulse, when an offence was either taken or given, at the very time that the heart of the chider or repulser was open before me, overflowing with esteem and affection; and the fair repulser dreading to be taken at her word, directing *this* word, or *that* expression, to be softened or changed. One, highly gratified with her lover's fervour and vows of everlasting love, has said, when I have asked her direction: 'I cannot tell you what to write; but (her heart on her lips) you cannot write too kindly.' All her fear only that she should incur slight for her kindness.

I recollect that I was early noted for having invention. I was not fond of play, as other boys: my schoolfellows used to call me 'Serious' and 'Gravity'. And five of them particularly delighted to single me out, either for a walk, or at their fathers' houses or at mine, to tell them stories, as they phrased it. Some I told them from my reading as true; others from my head, as mere invention; of which they would be most fond, and often were affected by them. One of them, particularly, I remember, was for putting me to write a history, as he called it, on the model of Tommy Potts. I now forget what it was; only, that it was of a servant-man preferred by a fine young lady (for his goodness) to a lord who was a libertine. All my stories carried with him, I am bold to say, a useful moral.

CHARLOTTE BRONTE

from *Jane Eyre*

All John Reed's violent tyrannies, all his sisters' proud indifference, all his mother's aversion, all the servants' partiality, turned up in my disturbed mind like a dark deposit in a turbid well. Why was I always suffering, always browbeaten, always accused, forever condemned?

Why could I never please? Why was it useless to try to win any one's favour? Eliza, who was headstrong and selfish, was respected. Georgiana, who had a spoiled temper, a very acrid spite, a captious and insolent carriage, was universally indulged. Her beauty, her pink cheeks, and golden curls, seemed to give delight to all who looked at her, and to purchase indemnity for every fault. John no one thwarted, much less punished, though he twisted the necks of the pigeons, killed the little pea-chicks, set the dogs at the sheep, stripped the hothouse vines of their fruit and broke the buds off the choicest plants in the conservatory; he called his mother 'old girl', too; sometimes reviled her for her dark skin, similar to his own; bluntly disregarded her wishes; not infrequently tore and spoiled her silk attire; and he was still 'her own darling'. I dared commit no fault; I strove to fulfil every duty; and I was termed naughty and tiresome, sullen and sneaking, from morning to noon, and from noon to night.

My head still ached and bled with the blow and fall I had received; no one had reproved John for wantonly striking me; and because I had turned against him to avert further irrational violence, I was loaded with general opprobrium.

'Unjust! – unjust!' said my reason, forced by the agonizing stimulus into precocious though transitory power; and Resolve, equally wrought up, instigated some strange expedient to achieve escape from insupportable oppression – as running away, or, if that could not be effected, never eating or drinking more, and letting myself die.

What a consternation of soul was mine that dreary afternoon! How all my brain was in tumult, and all my heart in insurrection! Yet in what darkness, what dense ignorance, was the mental battle fought! I could not answer the ceaseless inward question – *why* I thus suffered; now, at the distance of – I will not say how many years – I see it clearly.

I was a discord at Gateshead Hall; I was like nobody there; I had nothing in harmony with Mrs Reed or her children, or her chosen vassalage. If they did not love me, in fact, as little did I love them. They were not bound to regard with affection a thing that could not sympathize with one amongst them; a heterogeneous thing, opposed to them in temperament, in capacity, in propensities; a useless thing, incapable of serving their interests, or adding to their pleasure; a noxious thing, cherishing the germs of indignation at their treatment, of contempt of their judgement. I know that had I been a sanguine, brilliant, careless, exacting, handsome, romping child – though equally dependent and friendless – Mrs Reed would have endured my presence more complacently; her children would have entertained for me more of the cordiality of fellow feeling; the servants would have been less prone to make me the scapegoat of the nursery.

Daylight began to forsake the red room; it was past four o'clock, and the beclouded afternoon was tending to drear twilight. I heard the rain still beating continuously on the staircase window, and the wind howling in the grove behind the hall; I grew by degrees cold as a stone, and then my courage sank. My habitual mood of humiliation, self-doubt, forlorn depression, fell damp on the embers of my decaying ire. All said I was wicked, and perhaps I might be so: what thought had I been but just conceiving of starving myself to death? That certainly was a crime: and was I fit to die? Or was the vault under the chancel of Gateshead Church an inviting bourne? In such vault I had been told did Mr Reed lie buried; and led by this thought to recall his idea, I dwelt on it with gathering dread. I could not remember him, but I knew that he was my own uncle – my mother's brother – that he had taken me when a parentless infant to his house; and that in his last moments he had required a promise of Mrs Reed that she would rear and maintain me as one of her own children. Mrs Reed probably considered she had kept this promise; and so she had, I dare say, as well as her nature would permit her: but how could she really like an interloper, not of her race, and unconnected with her, after her husband's death, by any tie? It must have been most irksome to find herself bound by a hard-wrung pledge to stand in the stead of a parent to a strange child she could not love, and to see an uncongenial alien permanently intruded on her own family group.

A singular notion dawned upon me. I doubted not – never doubted – that if Mr Reed had been alive he would have treated me kindly; and now, as I sat looking at the white bed and overshadowed walls – occasionally also turning a fascinated eye towards the dimly gleaming mirror – I began to recall what I had heard of dead men, troubled in their graves by the violation of their last wishes, revisiting the earth to punish the perjured and avenge the oppressed; and I thought Mr Reed's spirit, harassed by the wrongs of his sister's child, might quit its abode – whether in the church vault or in the unknown world of the departed – and rise before me in this chamber. I wiped my tears and hushed my sobs, fearful lest any sign of violent grief might waken a preternatural voice to comfort me, or elicit from the gloom some haloed face, bending over me with strange pity. This idea, consolatory in theory, I felt would be terrible if realized: with all my might I endeavoured to stifle it – I endeavoured to be firm. Shaking my hair from my eyes, I lifted my head and tried to look boldly round the dark room; at this moment a light gleamed on the wall. Was it, I asked myself, a ray from the moon penetrating some aperture in the blind? No; moonlight was still, and this stirred; while I gazed, it glided up to the ceiling and quivered over my head. I can now conjecture readily that this streak of light was, in all likelihood, a gleam from a lantern carried by some one across the lawn; but then, prepared as my mind was for horror, shaken as my nerves were by agitation, I thought the swift-darting beam was a herald of some coming vision from another world. My heart beat thick, my head grew hot; a sound filled my ears, which I deemed the rushing of wings; something seemed near me; I was oppressed, suffocated; endurance broke down; I rushed to the door and shook the lock in desperate effort. Steps came running along the outer passage; the key turned, Bessie and Abbot entered.

'Miss Eyre, are you ill?' said Bessie.

'What a dreadful noise! It went quite through me!' exclaimed Abbot.

'Take me out! Let me go into the nursery!' was my cry.

'What for? Are you hurt? Have you seen something?' again demanded Bessie.

'Oh! I saw a light, and I thought a ghost would come.' I had now got hold of Bessie's hand, and she did not snatch it from me.

'She has screamed out on purpose,' declared Abbot, in some disgust. 'And what a scream! If she had been in great pain one would have excused it, but she only wanted to bring us all here; I know her naughty tricks.'

'What is all this?' demanded another voice peremptorily; and Mrs Reed came along the corridor, her cap flying wide, her gown rustling stormily. 'Abbot and Bessie, I believe I gave orders that Jane Eyre should be left in the red room till I came to her myself.'

'Miss Jane screamed so loud, ma'am,' pleaded Bessie.

'Let her go,' was the only answer. 'Loose Bessie's hands, child: you cannot succeed in getting out by these means, be assured. I abhor artifice, particularly in children; it is my duty to show you that tricks will not answer; you will now stay here an hour longer, and it is only on condition of perfect submission and stillness that I shall liberate you then.'

'Oh, aunt! have pity! Forgive me! I cannot endure it – let me be punished some other way! I shall be killed if—'

'Silence! This violence is almost repulsive'; and so, no doubt, she felt it. I was a precocious actress in her eyes: she sincerely looked on me as a compound of virulent passions, mean spirit, and dangerous duplicity.

Bessie and Abbot having retreated, Mrs Reed, impatient of my now frantic anguish and wild sobs, abruptly thrust me back and locked me in, without further parley. I heard her sweeping away; and soon after she was gone, I suppose I had a species of fit: unconsciousness closed the scene.

WILLIAM WORDSWORTH

My heart leaps up when I behold
   A rainbow in the sky:
So was it when my life began;
So is it now I am a man;
So be it when I shall grow old,
   Or let me die!
The Child is father of the Man;
And I could wish my days to be
Bound each to each by natural piety.

GRAHAM GREENE

from *The Power and the Glory*

There is always one moment in childhood when the door opens and lets the future in.

JAMAICA KINCAID

'Gwen'

On opening day, I walked to my new school alone. It was the first and last time that such a thing would happen. All around me were other people my age – twelve years – girls and boys, dressed in their school uniforms, marching off to school. They all seemed to know each other, and as they met they would burst into laughter, slapping each other on the shoulder and back, telling each other things that must have made for much happiness. I saw some girls wearing the same uniform as my own, and my heart just longed for them to say something to me, but the most they could do to include me was to smile and nod in my direction as they walked on arm in arm. I could hardly blame them for not paying more attention to me. Everything about me was so new: my uniform was new, my shoes were new, my hat was new, my shoulder ached from the weight of my new books in my new bag; even the road I walked on was new, and I must have put my feet down as if I weren't sure the ground was solid. At school, the yard was filled with more of these girls and their most sure-of-themselves gaits. When I looked at them, they made up a sea. They were walking in and out among the beds of flowers, all across the fields, all across the courtyard, in and out of classrooms. Except for me, no one seemed a stranger to anything or anyone. Hearing the way they greeted each other, I couldn't be sure that they hadn't all come out of the same woman's belly, and at the same time, too. Looking at them, I was suddenly glad that because I had wanted to avoid an argument with my mother I had eaten all my breakfast, for now I surely would have fainted if I had been in any more weakened a condition.

I knew where my classroom was, because my mother and I had kept an appointment at the school a week before. There I met some of my teachers and was shown the ins and outs of everything. When I saw it then, it was nice and orderly and empty and smelled just scrubbed. Now it smelled of girls milling around, fresh ink in inkwells, new books, chalk and erasers. The girls in my classroom acted even more familiar with each other. I was sure I would never be able to tell them apart just from looking at them, and I was sure that I would never be able to tell them apart from the sound of their voices.

When the school bell rang at half past eight, we formed ourselves into the required pairs and filed into the auditorium for morning prayers and hymn-singing. Our headmistress gave us a little talk, welcoming the new students and welcoming back the old students, saying that she hoped we had all left our bad ways behind us, that we would be good examples for each other and bring greater credit to our school than any of the other groups of girls who had been there before us. My palms were wet, and quite a few times the ground felt as if it were seesawing under my feet, but that didn't stop me from taking in a few things. For instance, the headmistress, Miss Moore. I knew right away that she had come to Antigua from England, for she looked like a prune left out of its jar a long time and she sounded as if she had borrowed her voice from an owl. The way she said, 'Now, girls . . .' When she was just standing still there, listening to some of the other activities, her grey eyes going all around the room hoping to see something wrong, her throat would beat up and down as if a fish fresh out of water were caught inside. I wondered if she even smelled like a fish. Once when I didn't wash, my mother had given me a long scolding about it, and she ended by saying that it was the only thing she didn't like about English people: they didn't wash often enough, or wash properly when they finally did. My mother had said, 'Have you ever noticed how they smell as if they had been bottled up in a fish?' On either side of Miss Moore stood our other teachers, women and men – mostly women. I recognized Miss George, our music teacher; Miss Nelson, our homeroom teacher; Miss Edward, our history and geography teacher; and Miss Newgate, our algebra and geometry teacher. I had met them the day my mother and I were at school. I did not know who the others were, and I did not worry about it. Since they were teachers, I was sure it wouldn't be long before, because of some misunderstanding, they would be thorns in my side.

We walked back to our classroom the same way we had come, quite orderly and, except for a few whispered exchanges, quite silent. But no sooner were we back in our classroom than the girls were in each other's laps, arms wrapped around necks. After peeping over my shoulder left and right, I sat down in my seat and wondered what would become of me. There were twenty of us in my class, and we were seated at desks arranged five in a row, four rows deep. I was at a desk in the third row, and this made me even more miserable. I hated to be seated so far away from the teacher, because I was sure I would miss something she said. But, even worse, if I was out of my teacher's sight all the time, how could she see my industriousness and quickness at learning things? And, besides, only dunces were seated so far to the rear, and I could not bear to be thought a dunce. I was now staring at the back of a shrubby-haired girl seated in the front row – the seat I most coveted, since it was directly in front of the teacher's desk. At that moment, the girl twisted herself around, stared at me, and said, 'You are Annie John? We hear you are very bright.' It was a good thing Miss Nelson walked in right then, for how would it have appeared if I had replied,

'Yes, that is completely true' – the very thing that was on the tip of my tongue.

As soon as Miss Nelson walked in, we came to order and stood up stiffly at our desks. She said to us, 'Good morning, class,' half in a way that someone must have told her was the proper way to speak to us and half in a jocular way, as if we secretly amused her. We replied, 'Good morning, Miss' in unison and in a respectful way, at the same time making a barely visible curtsy, also in unison. When she had seated herself at her desk, she said to us, 'You may sit now', and we did. She opened the roll book, and as she called out our names each of us answered, 'Present, Miss.' As she called out our names, she kept her head bent over the book, but when she called out my name and I answered with the customary response she looked up and smiled at me and said, 'Welcome, Annie.' Everyone, of course, then turned and looked at me. I was sure it was because they could hear the loud racket my heart was making in my chest.

It was the first day of a new term, Miss Nelson said, so we would not be attending to any of our usual subjects; instead, we were to spend the morning in contemplation and reflection and writing something she described as an 'autobiographical essay'. In the afternoon, we would read aloud to each other our autobiographical essays. (I knew quite well about 'autobiography' and 'essay', but reflection and contemplation! A day at school spent in such a way! Of course, in most books all the good people were always contemplating and reflecting before they did anything. Perhaps in her mind's eye she could see our future and, against all prediction, we turned out to be good people.) On hearing this, a huge sigh went up from the girls. Half the sighs were in happiness at the thought of sitting and gazing off into clear space, the other half in unhappiness at the misdeeds that would have to go unaccomplished. I joined the happy half, because I knew it would please Miss Nelson, and my own selfish interest aside, I liked so much the way she wore her ironed hair and her long-sleeved blouse and box-pleated skirt that I wanted to please her.

The morning was uneventful enough: a girl spilled ink from her inkwell all over her uniform; a girl broke her pen nib and then made a big to-do about replacing it; girls twisted and turned in their seats and pinched each other's bottoms; girls passed notes to each other. All this Miss Nelson must have seen and heard, but she didn't say anything – only kept reading her book: an elaborately illustrated edition of *The Tempest*, as later, passing by her desk, I saw. Midway in the morning we were told to go out and stretch our legs and breathe some fresh air for a few minutes; when we returned, we were given glasses of cold lemonade and a slice of bun to refresh us.

As soon as the sun stood in the middle of the sky, we were sent home for lunch. The earth may have grown an inch or two larger between the time I had walked to school that morning and the time I went home to lunch, for some girls made a small space for me in their little band. But I couldn't pay much attention to them; my mind was on my new surroundings, my new teacher, what I had written in my nice new notebook with its black-all-mixed-up-with-white cover and smooth lined pages (so glad was I to get rid of my old notebooks, which had on their covers a picture of a wrinkled-up woman wearing a crown on her head and a neckful and armfuls of diamonds and pearls – their pages so coarse, as if they were made of cornmeal). I flew home. I must have eaten my food. I flew back to school. By half past one, we were sitting under a flamboyant tree in a secluded part of our schoolyard, our autobiographical essays in hand. We were about to read aloud what we had written during our morning of contemplation and reflection.

In response to Miss Nelson, each girl stood up and read her composition. One girl told of a much revered and loved aunt who now lived in England and of how much she looked forward to one day moving to England to live with her aunt; one girl told of her brother studying medicine in

Canada and the life she imagined he lived there (it seemed quite odd to me); one girl told of the fright she had when she dreamed she was dead, and of the matching fright she had when she woke and found that she wasn't (everyone laughed at this, and Miss Nelson had to call us to order over and over); one girl told of how her oldest sister's best friend's cousin's best friend (it was a real rigmarole) had gone on a Girl Guide jamboree held in Trinidad and met someone who millions of years ago had taken tea with Lady Baden-Powell; one girl told of an excursion she and her father had made to Redonda, and of how they had seen some booby birds tending their chicks. Things went on in that way, all so playful, all so imaginative. I began to wonder about what I had written, for it was the opposite of playful and it was the opposite of imaginative. What I had written was heartfelt, and, except for the very end, it was all too true. The afternoon was wearing itself thin. Would my turn ever come? What should I do, finding myself in a world of new girls, a world in which I was not even near the center?

It was a while before I realized that Miss Nelson was calling on me. My turn at last to read what I had written. I got up and started to read, my voice shaky at first, but since the sound of my own voice had always been a calming potion to me, it wasn't long before I was reading in such a way that, except for the chirp of some birds, the hum of bees looking for flowers, the silvery rush-rush of the wind in the trees, the only sound to be heard was my voice as it rose and fell in sentence after sentence. At the end of my reading, I thought I was imagining the upturned faces on which were looks of adoration, but I was not; I thought I was imagining, too, some eyes brimming over with tears, but again I was not. Miss Nelson said that she would like to borrow what I had written to read for herself, and that it would be placed on the shelf with the books that made up our own class library, so that it would be available to any girl who wanted to read it. This is what I had written:

'When I was a small child, my mother and I used to go

down to Rat Island on Sundays right after church, so that I could bathe in the sea. It was at a time when I was thought to have weak kidneys and a bath in the sea had been recommended as a strengthening remedy. Rat Island wasn't a place many people went to anyway, but by climbing down some rocks my mother had found a place that nobody seemed to have ever been. Since this bathing in the sea was a medicine and not a picnic, we had to bathe without wearing swimming costumes. My mother was a superior swimmer. When she plunged into the seawater, it was as if she had always lived there. She would go far out if it was safe to do so, and she could tell just by looking at the way the waves beat if it was safe to do so. She could tell if a shark was near by, and she had never been stung by a jellyfish. I, on the other hand, could not swim at all. In fact, if I was in water up to my knees I was sure that I was drowning. My mother had tried everything to get me swimming, from using a coaxing method to just throwing me without a word into the water. Nothing worked. The only way I could go into the water was if I was on my mother's back, my arms clasped tightly around her neck, and she would then swim around not too far from the shore. It was only then that I could forget how big the sea was, how far down the bottom could be, and how filled up it was with things that couldn't understand a nice hallo. When we swam around in this way, I would think how much we were like the pictures of sea mammals I had seen, my mother and I, naked in the seawater, my mother sometimes singing to me a song in a French patois I did not yet understand, or sometimes not saying anything at all. I would place my ear against her neck, and it was as if I were listening to a giant shell, for all the sounds around me – the sea, the wind, the birds screeching – would seem as if they came from inside her, the way the sounds of the sea are in a seashell. Afterward, my mother would take me back to the shore, and I would lie there just beyond the farthest reach of a big wave and watch my mother as she swam and dove.

'One day, in the midst of watching my mother swim and dive, I heard a commotion far out at sea. It was three ships going by, and they were filled with people. They must have been celebrating something, for the ships would blow their horns and the people would cheer in response. After they passed out of view, I turned to look at my mother, but I could not see her. My eyes searched the small area of water where she should have been, but I couldn't find her. I stood up and started to call out her name, but no sound would come out of my throat. A huge black space then opened up in front of me and I fell inside it. I couldn't see what was in front of me and I couldn't hear anything around me. I couldn't think of anything except that my mother was no longer near me. Things went on in this way for I don't know how long. I don't know what, but something drew my eye in one direction. A little bit out of the area in which she usually swam was my mother, just sitting and tracing patterns on a large rock. She wasn't paying any attention to me, for she didn't know that I had missed her. I was glad to see her and started jumping up and down and waving to her. Still she didn't see me, and then I started to cry, for it dawned on me that, with all the water between us and I being unable to swim, my mother could stay there for ever and the only way I would be able to wrap my arms around her again was if it pleased her or if I took a boat. I cried until I wore myself out. My tears ran down into my mouth, and it was the first time that I realized tears had a bitter and salty taste. Finally, my mother came ashore. She was, of course, alarmed when she saw my face, for I had let the tears just dry there and they left a stain. When I told her what had happened, she hugged me so close that it was hard to breathe, and she told me that nothing could be farther from the truth – that she would never ever leave me. And though she said it over and over again, and though I felt better, I could not wipe out of my mind the feeling I had had when I couldn't find her.

'The summer just past, I kept having a dream about my mother sitting on the rock. Over and over I would have the dream – only in it my mother never came back, and sometimes my father would join her. When he joined her, they would both sit tracing patterns on the rock, and it must have been amusing, for they would always make each other laugh. At first, I didn't say anything, but when I began to have the dream again and again, I finally told my mother. Mother became instantly distressed; tears came to her eyes, and, taking me in her arms, she told me all the same things she had told me on the day at the sea, and this time the memory of the dark time when I felt I would never see her again did not come back to haunt me.'

I didn't exactly tell a lie about the last part. That is just what would have happened in the old days. But actually the past year saw me launched into young-ladyness, and when I told my mother of my dream – my nightmare, really – I was greeted with a turned back and a warning against eating certain kinds of fruit in an unripe state just before going to bed. I placed the old days' version before my classmates because, I thought, I couldn't bear to show my mother in a bad light before people who hardly knew her. But the real truth was that I couldn't bear to have anyone see how deep in disfavor I was with my mother.

As we walked back to the classroom, I in the air, my classmates on the ground, jostling each other to say some words of appreciation and congratulation to me, my head felt funny, as if it had swelled up to the size of, and weighed no more than, a blown-up balloon. Often I had been told by my mother not to feel proud of anything I had done and in the next breath that I couldn't feel enough pride about something I had done. Now I tossed from one to the other: my head bowed down to the ground, my head high up in the air. I looked at these girls surrounding me, my heart filled with just-sprung-up love, and I wished then and there to spend the rest of my life only with them.

As we approached our classroom, I felt a pinch on my arm. It was an affectionate pinch, I could tell. It was the girl who had earlier that day asked me if my name was Annie John. Now she told me that her name was Gweneth Joseph, and reaching into the pocket of her tunic, she brought out a small rock and presented it to me. She had found it, she said, at the foot of a sleeping volcano. The rock was black, and it felt rough in my hands, as if it had been through a lot. I immediately put it to my nose to see what it smelled like. It smelled of lavender, because Gweneth Joseph had kept it wrapped in a handkerchief doused in that scent. It may have been in that moment that we fell in love. Later, we could never agree on when it was. That afternoon, we walked home together, she going a little out of her usual way, and we exchanged likes and dislikes, our jaws dropping and eyes widening when we saw how similar they were. We separated ourselves from the other girls, and they, understanding everything, left us alone. We cut through a tamarind grove, we cut through a cherry-tree grove, we passed down the lane where all the houses had elaborate hedges growing in front, so that nothing was visible but the upstairs windows. When we came to my street, parting was all but unbearable. 'Tomorrow,' we said, to cheer each other up.

Gwen and I were soon inseparable. If you saw one, you saw the other. For me, each day began as I waited for Gwen to come by and fetch me for school. My heart beat fast as I stood in the front yard of our house waiting to see Gwen as she rounded the bend in our street. The sun, already way up in the sky so early in the morning, shone on her, and the whole street became suddenly empty so that Gwen and everything about her were perfect, as if she were in a picture. Her panama hat, with the navy blue and gold satin ribbon – our school colors – around the brim, sat lopsided on her head, for her head was small and she never seemed to get the correct-size hat, and it had to be anchored with a piece of elastic running under her chin. The pleats in the tunic of her uniform were in place, as was to be expected. Her cotton socks fit neatly around her ankles, and her shoes shone from just being polished. If a small breeze blew, it would ruffle the ribbons in her short, shrubby hair and the hem of her tunic; if the hem of her tunic was disturbed in that way, I would then be able to see her knees. She had bony knees and they were always ash-colored, as if she had just finished giving them a good scratch or had just finished saying her prayers. The breeze might also blow back the brim of her hat, and since she always walked with her head held down I might then be able to see her face: a small, flattish nose; lips the shape of a saucer broken evenly in two; wide, high cheekbones; ears pinned back close against her head – which was always set in a serious way, as if she were going over in her mind some of the many things we had hit upon that were truly a mystery to us. (Though once I told her that about her face, and she said that really she had only been thinking about me. I didn't look to make sure, but I felt as if my whole skin had become covered with millions of tiny red boils and that shortly I would explode with happiness.) When finally she reached me, she would look up and we would both smile and say softly, 'Hi.' We'd set off for school side by side, our feet in step, not touching but feeling as if we were joined at the shoulder, hip and ankle, not to mention heart.

As we walked together, we told each other things we had judged most private and secret: things we had overheard our parents say, dreams we had had the night before, the things we were really afraid of; but especially we told of our love for each other. Except for the ordinary things that naturally came up, I never told her about my changed feeling for my mother. I could see in what high regard Gwen held me, and I couldn't bear for her to see the great thing I had had once and then lost without an explanation. By the time we got to school, our chums often seemed overbearing, with their little comments on the well-pressedness of each other's uniforms, or on the neatness of their schoolbooks, or on how much they approved of the way Miss Nelson was wearing her hair these days. A few other girls were having much the same experience as Gwen and I, and when we heard comments of this kind we would look at each other and roll up our eyes and toss our hands in the air – a way of saying how above such concerns we were. The gesture was an exact copy, of course, of what we had seen our mothers do.

My life in school became just the opposite of my first morning. I went from being ignored, with hardly a glance from anyone, to having girls vie for my friendship, or at least for more than just a passing acquaintanceship. Both my classmates and my teachers noticed how quick I was at learning things. I was soon given responsibility for overseeing the class in the teacher's absence. At first, I was a little taken aback by this, but then I got used to it. I indulged many things, especially if they would end in a laugh or something touching. I would never dillydally with a decision, always making up my mind right away about the thing in front of me. Sometimes, seeing my old frail self in a girl, I would be heartless and cruel. It all went over quite well, and I became very popular.

My so recently much-hated body was now a plus: I excelled at games and was named captain of a volleyball team. As I was favored by my classmates inside and outside the classroom, so was I favored by my teachers – though only inside the classroom, for I had become notorious to them for doing forbidden things. If sometimes I stood away from myself and took a look at who I had become, I couldn't be more surprised at what I saw. But since who I had become earned me the love and devotion of Gwen and the other girls, I was only egged on to find new and better ways to entertain them. I don't know what invisible standard was set, or by whom or exactly when, but eight of us met it, and soon to the other girls we were something to comment on favorably or unfavorably, as the case might be.

It was a nook of some old tombstones – a place discovered by girls going to our school long before we were born – shaded by trees with trunks so thick it would take four arm's lengths to encircle them, that we would sit and talk about the things we said were on our minds that day. On our minds every day were our breasts and their refusal to budge out of our chests. On hearing somewhere that if a boy rubbed your breasts they would quickly swell up, I passed along this news. Since in the world we occupied and hoped for ever to occupy boys were banished, we had to make do with ourselves. What perfection we found in each other, sitting on these tombstones of long-dead people who had been the masters of our ancestors! Nothing in particular really troubled us except for the annoyance of a fly colliding with our lips, sticky from eating fruits; a bee wanting to nestle in our hair; the breeze suddenly blowing too strong. We were sure that the much-talked-about future that everybody was preparing us for would never come, for we had such a powerful feeling against it, and why shouldn't our will prevail this time? Sometimes when we looked at each other, it was all we could do not to cry out with happiness.

My own special happiness was, of course, with Gwen. She would stand in front of me trying to see into my murky black eyes – a way, she said, to tell exactly what I was thinking. After a short while, she would give up, saying, 'I can't make out a thing – only my same old face.' I would then laugh at her and kiss her on the neck, sending her into a fit of shivers, as if someone had exposed her to a cold draft when she had a fever. Sometimes when she spoke to me, so overcome with feeling would I be that I was no longer able to hear what she said, I could only make out her mouth as it moved up and down. I told her that I wished I had been named Enid, after Enid Blyton, the author of the first books I had discovered on my own and liked. I told her that when I was younger I had been afraid of my mother's dying, but that since I had met Gwen this didn't matter so much.

Whenever I spoke of my mother to her, I was always sure to turn the corners of my mouth down, to show my scorn. I said that I could not wait for us to grow up so that we could live in a house of our own. I had already picked out the house. It was a grey one, with many rooms, and it was in the lane where all the houses had high, well-trimmed hedges. With all my plans she agreed, and I am sure that if she had had any plans of her own I would have agreed with them also.

On the morning of the first day I started to menstruate, I felt strange in a new way – hot and cold at the same time, with horrible pains running up and down my legs. My mother, knowing what was the matter, brushed aside my complaints and said that it was all to be expected and I would soon get used to everything. Seeing my gloomy face, she told me in a half-joking way all about her own experience with the first step in coming of age, as she called it, which had happened when she was as old as I was. I pretended that this information made us close – as close as in the old days – but to myself I said, 'What a serpent!'

I walked to school with Gwen feeling as I supposed a dog must feel when it has done something wrong and is ashamed of itself and trying to get somewhere quick, where it can lie low. The cloth between my legs grew heavier and heavier with every step I took and I was sure that everything about me broadcast, 'She's menstruating today. She's menstruating today.' When Gwen heard what had happened, tears came to her eyes. She had not yet had the wonderful experience, and I could see that she cried for herself. She said that, in sympathy, she would wear a cloth, too.

In class, for the first time in my life, I fainted. Miss Nelson had to revive me, passing her smelling salts, which she had in a beautiful green vial, back and forth under my nose. She then took me to Nurse, who said that it was the fright of all the unexpected pain that had caused me to faint, but I knew that I had fainted after I brought to my mind a clear picture of myself sitting at my desk in my own blood.

At recess, among the tombstones, I of course had to exhibit and demonstrate. None of the others were menstruating yet. I showed everything without the least bit of flourish, since my heart wasn't in it. I wished instead that one of the other girls were in my place and that I were just sitting there in amazement. How nice they all were, though, rallying to my side, offering shoulders on which to lean, laps in which to rest my weary, aching head and kisses that really did soothe. When I looked at them sitting around me, the church in the distance, beyond that our school, with throngs of girls crossing back and forth in the schoolyard, beyond that the world, how I wished that everything would fall away, so that suddenly we'd be sitting in some different atmosphere, with no future full of ridiculous demands, no need for any sustenance save our love for each other, with no hindrance to any of our desires, which would of course, be simple desires – nothing, nothing, just sitting on our tombstones for ever. But that could never be, as the tolling of the school bell testified.

We walked back to class slowly, as if going to a funeral. Gwen and I vowed to love each other always, but the words had a hollow ring, and when we looked at each other we couldn't sustain the gaze. It had been decided by Miss Nelson and Nurse that I was not to return to school after lunch, with Nurse sending instructions to my mother to keep me in bed for the rest of the day.

When I got home, my mother came toward me, arms outstretched, concern written on her face. My whole mouth filled up with a bitter taste, for I could not understand how she could be so beautiful even though I no longer loved her.

JOHN MILTON

from *Paradise Regained*

The childhood shows the man,
As morning shows the day. Be famous then
By wisdom: as thy empire must extend,
So let extend thy mind o'er all the world.

THE CHILD REVISITED

THOMAS HOOD

from *I Remember*

I remember, I remember,
The fir trees dark and high;
I used to think their slender tops
Were close against the sky:
It was a childish ignorance,
But now 'tis little joy
To know I'm farther off from heav'n
Than when I was a boy.

WALTER DE LA MARE

'Myself'

There is a garden, grey
  With mists of autumntide;
Under the giant boughs,
  Stretched green on every side,

Along the lonely paths,
  A little child like me,
With face, with hands, like mine,
  Plays ever silently;

Oh, on, quite silently,
  When I am there alone,
Turns not his head; lifts not his eyes;
  Heeds not as he plays on.

After the birds are flown
  From singing in the trees,
When all is grey, all silent,
  Voices, and winds, and bees;

And I am there alone:
  Forlornly, silently,
Plays in the evening garden
  Myself with me.

SIEGFRIED SASSOON

'The Child at the Window'

Remember this, when childhood's far away;
The sunlight of a showery first spring day;
You from your house-top window laughing down,
And I, returned with whip-cracks from a ride,
On the great lawn below you, playing the clown.
Time blots our gladness out. Let this with love abide . . .

The brave March day; and you, not four years old,
Up in your nursery world – all heaven for me.
Remember this – the happiness I hold –
In far off springs I shall not live to see;
The world one map of wastening war unrolled,
And you, unconscious of it, setting my spirit free.

For you must learn, beyond bewildering years,
How little things beloved and held are best.
The windows of the world are blurred with tears,
And troubles come like cloud-banks from the west.
Remember this, some afternoon in spring,
When your own child looks down and makes your sad heart sing.

FERGAL KEANE

'Letter to Daniel'

My dear son, it is six o'clock in the morning on the island of Hong Kong. You are asleep cradled in my left arm and I am learning the art of one-handed typing. Your mother, more tired yet more happy than I've ever known her, is sound asleep in the room next door and there is soft quiet in our apartment.

Since you arrived, days have melted into night and back again and we are learning a new grammar, a long sentence whose punctuation marks are feeding and winding and nappy changing and these occasional moments of quiet.

When you're older we'll tell you that you were born in Britain's last Asian colony in the lunar year of the pig and that when we brought you home, the staff of our apartment block gathered to wish you well. 'It's a boy, so lucky, so lucky. We Chinese love boys,' they told us. One man said you were the first baby to be born in the block in the year of the pig. This, he told us, was good Feng Shui, in other words a positive sign for the building and everyone who lived there.

Naturally your mother and I were only too happy to believe that. We had wanted you and waited for you, imagined you and dreamed about you and now that you are here no dream can do justice to you. Outside the window, below us on the harbour, the ferries are ploughing back and forth to Kowloon. Millions are already up and moving about and the sun is slanting through the tower blocks and out on to the flat silver waters of the South China Sea. I can see the contrail of a jet over Lamma Island and, somewhere out there, the last stars flickering towards the other side of the world.

We have called you Daniel Patrick but I've been told by my Chinese friends that you should have a Chinese name as well and this glorious dawn sky makes me think we'll call you Son of the Eastern Star. So that later, when you and I are far from Asia, perhaps standing on a beach some evening, I can point at the sky and tell you of the Orient and the times and the people we knew there in the last years of the twentieth century.

Your coming has turned me upside down and inside out. So much that seemed essential to me has, in the past few days, taken on a different colour. Like many foreign correspondents I know, I have lived a life that, on occasion, has veered close to the edge: war zones, natural disasters, darkness in all its shapes and forms.

In a world of insecurity and ambition and ego, it's easy to be drawn in, to take chances with our lives, to believe that what we do and what people say about us is reason enough to gamble with death. Now, looking at your sleeping face, inches away from me, listening to your occasional sigh and gurgle, I wonder how I could have ever thought glory and prizes and praise were sweeter than life.

And it's also true that I am pained, perhaps haunted is a better word, by the memory, suddenly so vivid now, of each suffering child I have come across on my journeys. To tell you the truth, it's nearly too much to bear at this moment to even think of children being hurt and abused and killed. And yet looking at you, the images come flooding back. Ten-year-old Andi Mikail dying from napalm burns on a hillside in Eritrea, how his voice cried out, growing ever more faint when the wind blew dust on to his wounds. The two brothers, Domingo and Juste, in Menongue, southern Angola. Juste, two years old and blind, dying from malnutrition, being carried on seven-year-old Domingo's back. And Domingo's words to me, 'He was nice before, but now he has the hunger.'

Last October, in Afghanistan, when you were growing inside your mother, I met Sharja, aged twelve. Motherless, fatherless, guiding me through the grey ruins of her home, everything was gone, she told me. And I knew that, for all her tender years, she had learned more about loss than I would likely understand in a lifetime.

There is one last memory. Of Rwanda, and the churchyard of the parish of Nyarabuye where, in a ransacked classroom, I found a mother and her three young children huddled together where they'd been beaten to death. The children had died holding on to their mother, that instinct we all learn from birth and in one way or another cling to until we die.

Daniel, these memories explain some of the fierce protectiveness I feel for you, the tenderness and the occasional moments of blind terror when I imagine anything happening to you. But there is something more, a story from long ago that I will tell you face to face, father to son, when you are older. It's a very personal story but it's part of the picture. It has to do with the long lines of blood and family, about our lives and how we can get lost in them and, if we're lucky, find our way out again into the sunlight.

It begins thirty-five years ago in a big city on a January morning with snow on the ground and a woman walking to hospital to have her first baby. She is in her early twenties and the city is still strange to her, bigger and noisier than the easy streets and gentle hills of her distant home. She's walking because there is no money and everything of value has been pawned to pay for the alcohol to which her husband has become addicted.

On the way, a taxi driver notices her sitting, exhausted and cold, in the doorway of a shop and he takes her to hospital for free. Later that day, she gives birth to a baby boy and, just as you are to me, he is the best thing she has ever seen. Her husband comes that night and weeps with joy when he sees his son. He is truly happy. Hungover, broke, but in his own way happy, for they were both young and in love with each other and their son.

But, Daniel, time had some bad surprises in store for them. The cancer of alcoholism ate away at the man and he lost his family. This was not something he meant to do or wanted to do, it just was. When you are older, my son, you will learn about how complicated life becomes, how we can lose our way and how people get hurt inside and out. By the time his son had grown up, the man lived away from the family, on his own in a one-roomed flat, living and dying for the bottle.

He died on the fifth of January, one day before the anniversary of his son's birth, all those years before in that snowbound city. But his son was too far away to hear his last words, his final breath, and all the things they might have wished to say to one another were left unspoken.

Yet now, Daniel, I must tell you that when you let out your first powerful cry in the delivery room of the Adventist Hospital and I became a father, I thought of your grandfather and, foolish though it may seem, hoped that in some way he could hear, across the infinity between the living and the dead, your proud statement of arrival. For if he could hear, he would recognize the distinct voice of family, the sound of hope and new beginnings that you and all your innocence and freshness have brought to the world.

WILLIAM SHAKESPEARE

from *As You Like It*

JAQUES All the world's a stage,
And all the men and women merely players;
They have their exits and their entrances,
And one man in his time plays many parts,
His acts being seven ages. At first the infant,
Mewling and puking in the nurse's arms.
Then the whining school-boy with his satchel
And shining morning face, creeping like snail
Unwillingly to school. And then the lover,
Sighing like furnace, with a woeful ballad
Made to his mistress' eyebrow. Then a soldier,
Full of strange oaths, and bearded like the pard,
Jealous in honour, sudden, and quick in quarrel,
Seeking the bubble reputation
Even in the canon's mouth. And then the justice,
In fair round belly, with good capon lin'd,
With eyes severe, and beard of formal cut,
Full of wise saws, and modern instances,
And so he plays his part. The sixth age shifts
Into the lean and slipper'd pantaloon,
With spectacles on nose, and pouch on side,
His youthful hose well sav'd, a world too wide,
For his shrunk shank, and his big manly voice,
Turning again toward childish treble pipes,
And whistles in his sound. Last scene of all,

That ends this strange eventful history,
Is second childishness and mere oblivion,
Sans teeth, sans eyes, sans taste, sans every thing.

JENNY DISKI

from *Skating to Antarctica*

I took my time about using the information I had found in the porter's office. It was a couple of weeks before I looked up the names Rosen and Levine in the phone book and found their numbers, and a while after that before I picked up the phone. I called Mrs Rosen who, according to the directory, did indeed live next door but one to the fifth-floor flat I had lived in. If it was the same woman, Jonathan's mother – could it possibly be? – then she would have been my neighbour.

I introduced myself as Jenny Diski and explained who my parents were and which flat we had lived in. I then reintroduced myself in the silence. 'Jenny Diski – Jenny Simmonds, I used to play with Jonathan. You are Jonathan's mother, aren't you?'

That was when she said 'Jennifer', and I felt an odd wooziness come over me. I almost said no, not recognizing myself by that name. But I had been Jennifer when I was small, though for the life of me I only really remember being Jenny. I said yes, but felt fraudulent, which was curious because I never really like being called Jenny. *Diski* feels more accurately like me, though it is an entirely invented name to which both Roger-the-Ex and I changed on a whim when we got married. There was a gasp and then a brief silence.

'How are you?'

I was eleven when she had last known me, but what else was there to say?

'I'm well, thank you.'

I explained that I was a writer these days and was thinking about doing a book in part about my mother, that I didn't know anyone who knew us when we were a family at Paramount Court; would it be possible for me to come and talk to her, to get, as it were, an outside view of what went on?

'You and Jonathan were at the same school. Your mother and I took both of you the first day, you were only four. You went in quite happily. She cried when you'd gone. We went for a cup of coffee.'

My mother cried. Lord, she did love me. Then again, she would be on her own when I was at school. Cried for herself, probably. Leave it for later.

'Mrs Levine and Mrs Gold are still here. Do you remember Helen Levine and Marianne Gold, you used to play together? You're a writer you say? You're all right, then?'

'Yes. I'd really like to come and talk to you about my parents.'

There was an awkward pause. I liked the sound of her voice. London Jewish, parents foreign-speaking, brought up in the East End. She sounded alert and thoughtful; you could hear her remembering and considering what she remembered.

'Well, we were friends of your mother, of course. But . . . I'm afraid you didn't have a very happy childhood.' This last was said hesitantly, telling me there were things she thought I'd better not know.

'No, it was a bit of a mess, wasn't it?'

'Oh, you remember it, do you? You had a terrible time. I thought you would have forgotten. Well, in that case . . .'

I established that I wanted to know what had gone on from her – a contemporary adult's – point of view, and that I wasn't at all sensitive about what she had to tell me.

She seemed encouraged by that, and we arranged a date a few days off when I could come round to tea.

I was thrown by Mrs Rosen's genuine surprise that I recollected my childhood as being less than classically happy. At first I wondered if the idea of false memory syndrome had seeped deeper into the general consciousness than I had supposed. Why would I have blanked out what she seemed to remember? Because I couldn't stand to remember it, would be the post-Freudian supposition. But more likely the source of her surprise was the pre-Freudian notion that children are not really conscious entities. A comforting thought this for parents who can manage it. Odd how the modern notion of repressed memory syndrome fits with this more archaic formulation of childhood. What the pre- and post-Freudians have in common is the desire to believe children suppress unhappiness. Either it washes over them, or it washes under them. Take your choice. Either way, knowing clearly what happened isn't on the cards.

The sound of my parents fighting in our two-roomed flat on the third floor echoed through the corridors of Paramount Court, my father leaving several times, my mother being stretchered away to hospital, the furniture and fittings being confiscated by debt collectors when we were on the fifth floor: these were all public events, but somehow, it was assumed, I wouldn't retain a memory of those things. Adults experience, children don't. Enter Freud, announcing that even pre-conscious infants can experience, but still the idea of suppression held sway. They remember, but don't know they remember. Still, children and their experience are divorced from each other. Either way, parents have an opt-out, in the first case for life, in the second, until their offspring lie down on the psychiatrist's couch. Then the new, paid 'parent' brings it all back to them in vivid feelovision and well, everything's all right again. I recall my mother and father complaining about my firstly nervous and then wayward behaviour, as if what happened between them had nothing to do with me. 'Why are you like this?' they'd demand, outraged and genuinely puzzled that I should be so difficult. 'Oh, you remember, do you?' said Mrs Rosen.

Well, I remembered all sorts of things, and some of them the sort of thing you are supposed to keep hidden from your adult self, but what I lacked was corroboration and background. Neither of my parents told clear stories about themselves, most of the stuff I knew about them (as opposed to what I *knew* happened between them) came from the outbursts designed to give pain or pay back a bad deed: 'Now, I'll tell you the truth . . .' The truth was always unpleasant and about the other partner, it always upturned some previous cover story, and it was told as revelation, with the purpose of enlightening me as to the true nature of the monster who was one of my parents. The truth was dangerous, the truth was poison. The phrase 'Now, I'll tell you the truth . . .' made me flinch, knowing something was going to be said that would never be unsaid, and would live inside my head whether I wanted it or not. Neither of my parents, I came to understand, told the truth about themselves, only about each other, and the truth was never something to look forward to. As a result, I think, I've never respected the truth very much. It came and went according to emotions and in the end just told another, different story from the previous story.

The *truth* – she would tell me – was that my father had been in prison when I was very small and my mother had covered up the fact so I wouldn't think less of him. The *truth* – she would announce – was that my father's son by his first marriage had been killed, not, as they had previously told me, getting off a bus on the way home from school and being run over by the one behind, but running out of the house during a fight between his parents and falling under an oncoming bus. The *truth* – she'd declare – was that my father left my mother and me alone till all hours of the night, even when I was ill, because he was carrying on with some woman or other. The *truth* – the truth that she concealed but now would reveal to me – was that my father did not love me as he said he did, was a bastard and a crook and a coward.

The *truth* – my father would tell me – was that my mother had never had a breakdown when she was carried out of the flat after he left, but had faked it in order to get attention and to make my father return to her. The *truth* – he announced – was that her first husband came back from the war and was grateful to my father for taking my mother off his hands. The *truth* – he said – was that my mother drank, gambled and had no interest in anything but the spending of money. The *truth* – he disclosed – was that she insisted on being made unconscious when she gave birth to me, that she refused to touch me to change my napppies and that my father had had to do it. The *truth* – he told me – was that my mother had taken my father to court for my custody only as a ploy to get regular alimony and she had offered a deal before the session started whereby he could have me if she could have a fiver a week. The *truth* – he revealed – was that my mother and Pam, the woman my father was living with, made a deal before I went to live with my father at twelve to ensure that she would treat me in such a way that I would be unhappy there and want to return to my mother.

Between his truths about her and her truths about him were their truths about me. Mostly these were to do with me being dangerously like her (he said) or dangerously like him (she said). Mad, bad, evil, heartless, lazy, hard, undisciplined, inadequate, self-centred. Sometimes, like an opera, their rows would rage above my head and then precipitate down, suddenly including me. *And what about you?* I just sat there and listened, I didn't care, I thought it was funny, I was on his side, I was on her side. WHOSE SIDE WAS I ON? Eventually, this question would come up and seem to bring them together. They would both turn to look at me and genuinely expect an answer. Sometimes I played the little judge and said which argument seemed the most just; sometimes I mumbled that I didn't know; sometimes I just stayed shtoom. It didn't matter, all hell would rain down on my head whichever answer I gave or none.

All this was *truth*. Truth, I learned, was up for grabs, entirely dependent on who was doing the telling. Truth was something that happened secretly in the back of people's minds and came out of those minds like exploding sewage when there was enough anger or fear to impel it. Two things I learned from this: be very wary of the truth, and try to keep tabs on what is in the back of your own mind. Keep checking on what is there, don't let it seep into dark corners, loitering unseen until suddenly it jumps out at you. Know what you know. And try and know what others know, keep a check on their dark corners, never mind how ugly or improbable. It's a kind of armour against the rapier words. Never let yourself be surprised.

THE FIRST EPISTLE OF PAUL THE APOSTLE TO THE CORINTHIANS

'When I was a Child . . .'

When I was a child, I spake as a child, I understood as a child, I thought as a child: but when I became a man, I put away childish things.

For now we see through a glass, darkly; but then face to face: now I know in part; but then shall I know even as also I am known.

And now abideth faith, hope, charity, these three; but the greatest of these is charity.

ACKNOWLEDGEMENTS

The editor and publishers wish to thank the following for permission to use copyright material:

Bloodaxe Books for Maura Dooley, 'Freight' from *Kissing a Bone* (1996);

Curtis Brown Ltd, New York, on behalf of the Estate of the author for Ogden Nash, 'Baby, What Makes the Sky Blue?' from *The Face is Familiar*, Little Brown & Co. (1940). © 1940 by Ogden Nash, renewed;

Constable Publishers for Su Tung-P'o, 'On the Birth of His Son' from Arthur Waley, trans., *170 Chinese Poems* (1919);

Faber & Faber Ltd for an extract from Alan Bennett, *Forty Years On*;

Farrar, Straus and Giroux, Inc. for Isaac Bashevis Singer, 'Why I Write for Children' from *Nobel Lecture*. © 1978 by The Nobel Foundation;

A. M. Heath on behalf of the Estate of the author for Edna St Vincent Millay, 'Childhood is the Kingdom Where Nobody Dies';

David Higham Associates on behalf of the Estates of the authors for extracts from Dylan Thomas, *Portrait of the Artist as a Young Dog*, J. M. Dent; and Graham Greene, *The Power and the Glory*, William Heineman;

Macmillan General Books for extracts from Mary Karr, *The*

Liar's Club, Picador (1995): and with Schocken Books, distributed by Pantheon Books, a division of Random House Inc., for Binjamin Wilkomirski, *Fragments: Memories of a Childhood, 1939–1948*, trans. Carol Brown Janeway. © 1995 Binjamin Wilkomirski, translation © 1996 by Carol Brown Janeway;

Penguin UK for an extract from Elspeth Barker, *O Caledonia* Hamish Hamilton (1991);

Peters Fraser & Dunlop Group Ltd on behalf of the author for Michael Rosen, 'Song, A Playground Rhyme By Girls Aged Seven, London' from *Rude Rhymes*, Signet (1992); and on behalf of the Estate of the author for an extract from Hilaire Belloc, 'Jim, Who Ran Away From His Nurse' from *Cautionary Verses*, Random House UK;

John Murray (Publishers) Ltd for an extract from John Betjeman, 'Summoned by Bells';

Polygon for Liz Lochhead, 'Everybody's Mother' from *Dreaming Frankenstein & Collected Poems* (1984);

Random House UK for an extract from Christy Brown, *My Left Foot*, Secker & Warburg (1954);

Rogers Coleridge & White Ltd on behalf of the authors for extracts from Fergal Keane, 'Letter to Daniel' from *Letter to Daniel: Dispatches from the Heart*, Penguin Books, BBC Books (1996). © Fergal Keane 1996; Anita Desai, 'Games at Twilight' from *Games at Twilight and Other Stories*, William Heinemann (1978). © 1978 Anita Desai; and Adrian Henri, 'For Beauty Douglas' from *Collected Poems 1953–79*, Alison & Busby (1982). © Adrian Henri 1982;

George Sassoon for Siegfried Sassoon, 'The Child at the Window' from *Collected Poems* (1947);

The Society of Authors on behalf of the Literary Trustees of the author for Walter de la Mare, 'Keep Innocency', 'The Sleeping Child' and 'Myself' from *The Complete Poems of*

Walter de la Mare (1969); and as Literary Representative of the Estate of the author for A. E. Housman, 'The Grizzly Bear is Huge and Wild';

Virago Press for an extract from Alice Miller, *The Drama of Being a Child* (1987);

The Wylie Agency on behalf of the author for Jamaica Kincaid, 'Gwen', first published in *The New Yorker*. © 1994 Jamaica Kincaid;

Every effort has been made to trace the copyright holders but if any have been inadvertently overlooked the publishers will be pleased to make the necessary arrangement at the first opportunity.